THE
BRUTE

a novel by
MIKE KLAASSEN

Blue Works
Port Orchard, Washington

The Brute
copyright 2005 by Michael John Klaassen
published by Blue Works

ISBN 978-1-59092-225-5
9 8 7 6 5 4 3 2
First edition September 2005

Cover by Aron Dittbrenner.
Design by Blue Artisans Design.
Blue Card™ concept by Grace M. Garcia.
Ratings Block™ concept by Grace M. Garcia

For information about film, reprint or other subsidiary rights, please contact:
legal@windstormcreative.com

Blue Works is an imprint of Windstorm Creative, a multi-division, international organization involved in publishing books in all genres, including electronic publications; producing games, toys, videos and audio cassettes as well as producing theatre, film and visual arts events. The wind with the gear center was designed by Buster Blue of Blue Artisans Design and is a trademark of Blue Works.

Blue Works
c/o Windstorm Creative
7419 Ebbert Dr SE
Port Orchard, WA 98367
www.windstormcreative.com
360-769-7174

Blue Works is a member of the Orchard Creative Group, Ltd.

Library of Congress Cataloging in Publication Data available.

Dedication

Dedicated to my loving grandmother
Margaret Emilie Klaassen
who taught me so many things,
including how to butcher chickens.

Acknowledgments

Writing this novel, my first, has been an exciting and challenging journey that would not have been possible without the inspiration and support of my wife, Carol.

I'm also grateful for the other help I've received along the way. Thanks go to the Institute of Children's Literature *Writing for Children and Teenagers* course for providing a starting point, and to *Writer's Digest* magazine and book club for numerous articles and books about writing.

Acknowledgements also go to the following for their helpful comments and encouragement: children's-book-reviewer Steve Johnson; Ron Smith of Wichita State University; Richard Irby of Valley Center High School; author Paul Bagdon; and self-employed-editor Laurie Rosin.

I also appreciate the dedicated team at Windstorm Creative for bringing this tale to publication.

THE
BRUTE

a novel by
MIKE KLAASSEN

CHAPTER
ONE

A crack of thunder jolted Fortney Curtis from his sleep. Lightning flashed outside his tent, and the ground seemed to buck beneath him. The storm generated an eerie symphony of light and sound that made him think of ancient Greek gods battling in the sky.

Fort had been through Kansas thunderstorms on campouts before, and they usually passed by quickly. Still, the intensity of this one made him shiver and burrow more deeply into his sleeping bag. He pulled the top over his head, leaving a small opening just big enough so he could see and breathe. A light, refreshing smell caught his attention. He recognized it as ozone, the smell of rain. Or was it actually the smell of lightning?

His father and Mr. Crawford, the Scoutmaster, were probably calmly observing the light show from their own tent, but Fort was sure the six younger Boy Scouts, including his eleven-year-old twin brothers, must be terrified.

The thought of the younger Scouts made his

forehead throb. He had promised he would control his temper, but that morning, at the Newton Ranch headquarters, he had lost his cool and slugged one of his little brothers. Fort remembered the flash of anger and disappointment in his father's eyes.

To make matters worse, he had socked his little brother in front of Tana Newton, the ranch owner's niece. His face flushed in spite of the cool night air, and he wiped beads of sweat from his forehead. He pictured Tana on her horse at the ranch house—white cowboy hat over her long brown hair, brown eyes sparkling, and a teasing smile on her friendly face.

Just thinking about her made his insides ache. Their fingers had touched momentarily, and electricity had coursed through him. He couldn't wait to see her again, to get to know her, to touch her, to . . . .

Then it hit him. He had probably ruined any chance with her. Most of the girls at school avoided him—even considered him dangerous. His size and muscular build, together with his violent temper, had earned him a nickname: The Brute.

He squirmed. He wasn't a bad person, but sometimes even little things set him off on a rampage. He tried hard to control himself, but sometimes the unexpected would set him off. The thought of really hurting someone filled him with dread, and he assumed that somehow, somewhere, he would be punished. He wished he could fall back to sleep so he wouldn't think about his temper any more.

Rain plopped on the tent, the sound gradually increasing to a numbing roar. The roof bent downward, and for a moment Fort feared his shelter would collapse around him. Then, as suddenly as it had started, the rain quit. Maybe the storm had passed. Good. Still, they would have to cook breakfast and break camp in the mud tomorrow.

Just last week he had told his mom and dad that he was thinking about dropping out of the Boy Scouts. "I'm the only guy left in the troop who's my age, the meetings bore me, and I'm tired of going on campouts every month," he had complained.

"But, Son," his dad had pleaded, "Mr. Crawford and I are starting a new troop, and we're counting on your help. Besides, you're so close to becoming an Eagle Scout. Can't you stick with it a little longer?"

Fort had agreed—reluctantly. Now he was camping with six new Scouts along a remote, wooded creek on the Newton ranch in the Flint Hills of Kansas. Just as Fort's former troop had done, these new Scouts had pitched their tents out of sight of the adults, far enough away to have a sense of being on their own, but close enough to seek help if they needed it.

10 THE BRUTE

Fort hadn't relished the thought of hot, eleven-year-old bodies crowding him all night, so he had set up a tent for himself. Feeling his feet touching the back of it while his head pressed against the nylon canvas door, he figured he took up the same space as two of the smaller boys. His oversized body was handy on the football field, but a real nuisance in a small tent.

For a few seconds he listened to the patter of water dripping from the trees to the wet ground outside. The lulling sound was interrupted by a sharp thump that sounded like a rock hitting a tree.

He wondered if his brothers were teasing him again—as they had for most of the afternoon. Fort was still disgusted with them for horsing around while he tried to show them how to set up camp and cook dinner. Then they had dawdled over washing the dishes, not finishing until just before dark.

He smiled in the darkness at the thought of paying them back. Maybe he would sneak up behind their tents and growl, to scare them so badly they wouldn't be able to sleep for the rest of the night. It would serve the little pests right. Then he frowned at the thought of crawling around in the mud. No. He would stay in his nice warm sleeping bag and howl like a coyote. He cupped his hands around his mouth and took a deep breath.

Before he could make a sound, he heard another object slap through the branches above, then splash into a puddle. Hail, he realized, as a roaring barrage of ice balls pelted the tent, its roof whipping from side to side. He covered his head, fearing the tent would be ripped to shreds. After a few harrowing moments, the wind lessened, and the hail petered out.

He unzipped the sleeping bag, switched on his flashlight, and zipped the tent door open. Hailstones the size of golf balls carpeted the wet ground. He grabbed some of the ice and pulled it back into the tent.

Fort studied the cold, wet hailstones in his hand. One was broken in half. He could see ice rings, some white, some almost clear, and then he wondered why the concentric layers were different colors. His hand was getting numb from the cold, so he tossed the hailstones back out into the mud, zipped the tent door shut, slipped into his sleeping bag, and stared at the sagging tent ceiling.

He wondered what his buddies from the wrestling and football teams were doing tonight. Probably out on dates. The thought of asking a girl out for a date gave him a nervous ache in his stomach.

Now that he was sixteen, he could drive his parents' automobiles. He wished he could buy his own car, but his mom and dad had discouraged him from getting a job during the school year. Two more years of high school, he figured, and he could leave home and do whatever he wanted. Some of his friends had already picked out careers, or thought they had. Fort had no idea what he wanted to do when he finished school. He stared into the darkness of his tent, wishing he could fall asleep again.

A faint noise caught his attention, and he strained to hear. After a moment he realized that one of the younger boys was crying. Little wimp. He pulled the edge of the sleeping bag over his head so he wouldn't hear the sobbing, but the sound kept nagging at his mind. Then he remembered his own first campout. He had been so spooked that he had climbed into his dad's tent for the night.

Fort rolled onto his back and tugged the edge of the sleeping bag off his head. He could still hear the crying, and now he recognized the voice. No surprise.

"Billy?" he asked, in a voice he hoped was loud enough to carry to the next tent.

The crying stopped but there was no answer.

"Billy, are you okay?"

"I'm scared," said a young voice.

"Just roll over and close your eyes," said Fort. "You'll fall asleep. Before you know it, it'll be morning."

The sobbing continued as Fort lay on his back staring into the darkness. He could picture his twin brothers in the tent with Billy. They were probably sound asleep with their bags over their heads, oblivious to Billy's crying.

"Billy. Listen to me." The crying grew faint. "Do you want to come over here?"

A moment of silence passed before Fort heard a weak reply. "Okay."

"Well, then, come on over," said Fort. He listened for the sound of the boy gathering his stuff and unzipping the tent. Nothing.

"Billy? Are you coming over or not?"

Fort could hear more sobbing.

"Billy, what are you scared of? Just grab your sleeping bag and walk on over!"

"Can you come get me?"

Fort felt like yelling, but figured that wouldn't help the situation. He considered just leaving Billy where he was, but the little boy might cry all night. Then neither one of them would get any sleep.

Muttering under his breath, Fort crawled out of the sleeping bag, found his flashlight, and unzipped the tent. The air was heavy with moisture. A gust of wind howled through the trees, making him shiver. He was wearing only his white-cotton briefs and wondered if he should have put on his pants. Cold mud squished up between his toes. As he splashed toward Billy's tent, something stabbed into the tender arch of his bare foot. He cursed and limped toward the tents ahead of him, trying to avoid sticks and rocks.

He could see two tents and knew each contained three boys. Approaching the nearest one he whispered, "Billy?"

The boy answered, and Fort could hear rustling sounds from within. He unzipped the tent and peeked inside. As he had suspected, his brothers were burrowed deep in their bags. Billy squinted and blinked at the flashlight. Seeing the boy reminded Fort of his mother's reaction to Billy.

"That little Billy Stockton is so cute with those blue eyes and blond hair. I just want to pick him up and hug him every time I see him," she had said.

Fort would not admit it, but he envied the younger boy. With Fort's rough features, he knew nobody ever referred to him as cute, or even handsome. People who liked him tended to call him rugged-looking. Others just called him scary—although never to his face. As the slender boy coughed and wiped his eyes, Fort had to admit it would be hard not to like Billy.

They squished their way through the mud again, carrying Billy's sleeping bag. Fort helped Billy get settled and wiped the mud off his own feet before slipping back into his own bag. He could see an expression of relief on Billy's face.

"Thanks, Fort." Billy snuggled into the bag and closed his eyes.

Fort rolled so his back was to Billy, then pulled the top of the bag up around his cheeks and settled in for what he hoped would be an uninterrupted few hours of sleep, but he felt Billy rustle behind him. The boy leaned over Fort's shoulder.

"Fort, I don't feel good."

Fort blinked a couple of times before answering. "Just lie down and go to sleep. You'll be fine in the morning."

At first, Fort didn't recognize the sound, a combination of gagging and gushing fluid. But he instantly recognized the sour smell—vomit. He sat up, completely awake, and switched on his flashlight just in time to see Billy spewing greenish-brown liquid over their sleeping bags. Fort could identify chunks of partially digested beef, potatoes, and carrots as they flowed onto the tent floor.

Billy spat a couple of times, then wiped his mouth with the sleeve of his shirt. "Sorry," he said, and then started to sob.

Fort cringed. He felt like throwing Billy out into the

mud. Instead, he grabbed a towel. "It's okay, Billy."

That does it, he thought as he began cleaning the sleeping bags, I'm not going on any more campouts. He noticed the gray-and-brown camouflage pattern of his pants at the edge of the tent and checked them for vomit, then did the same for his red baseball cap. After he had wiped away most of the puke, he tossed the towel outside.

The inside of the tent reeked, and Fort considered taking his sleeping bag to his dad's vehicle and spending the night there. Then he heard a low-pitched, rhythmic sound and realized that Billy was snoring. He suddenly felt very tired, laid back down, and was almost asleep when another noise caught his attention.

It started in the distance and intensified: a vibration like a bass guitar turned up really loud. The vibration amplified to a roar, like a jet flying low overhead, or a fast-moving train. Suddenly, he knew what he was hearing. His mind screamed at him to run and take cover somewhere, anywhere, but fear held him like a straightjacket. His insides seemed to melt. He couldn't move or scream.

The roar grew deeper and louder until it rumbled through the earth under him and resonated through his bones. Over the deep roar he could hear a high-pitched howling wind that tore at his ears until his teeth ached. In his mind he could see a giant, rotating funnel bearing down on him in the darkness.

The tent snapped from side to side, then collapsed. The shrieking wind pummeled Fort through the thin nylon canvas. As the flattened tent flipped over, it hurled him up and then dropped him to the ground, pounding the wind out of him. He heard Billy scream. Before Fort could reach for him, the tent began to roll, and they tumbled helplessly inside it.

Fort's stomach ached as the tent fabric plastered against his face, suffocating him. Gasping and clawing at the canvas, he could feel himself being propelled upward with incredible speed. He tried to scream, but no sound came. He tried to reach out to find Billy, but his arms wouldn't move. He plunged downward, then up, rolling and spinning over and over again.

Then everything slowed. He could still hear the powerful, rushing roar, but it seemed farther away. The tent fabric loosened its clinging hold on his face and body, and he could breathe again. The canvas fluttered and flapped. He stretched his arms and legs, feeling weightless, like an astronaut floating freely in a space capsule. For a split second, time and motion stopped—a carefree sensation, so different from the horror of moments earlier.

18 THE BRUTE

In an instant, the sensation of weightlessness evaporated. He was falling. His stomach seemed to hang in his mouth with that horrible roller-coaster sensation. He screamed, arms thrashing, grasping for something to stop the fall. He felt Billy, still wrapped in his bag, and clutched the boy to his chest. In a flash, he imagined both of them on the ground, dead, a bloody pile of broken bones and guts splattered around the inside of the tent. A sad, gory end to their young lives.

Then something solid whacked Fort's back with the force of a baseball bat. He tumbled head over heels as he was hit repeatedly. The tent bounced up, then sideways, then down again. Something dense and hard pounded his side. Again he fell and was stabbed by dozens of sticks jabbing at him through the tent. He tumbled sideways onto more poking sticks. He rolled and fell again, with a crushing thud. Solid ground.

CHAPTER TWO

Fort lay stunned, nauseated, and breathless as tree limbs snapped and debris crashed through the trees. He rolled until he covered Billy, protecting both of their heads with his arms. The sleeping bags and tent made a flimsy cocoon around them as the storm howled overhead.

The wind finally eased, then grew still. In the spooky silence he strained for any sound, but heard only the light patter of rain.

Pain brought Fort's attention back to himself. His entire body throbbed. Still numb and disoriented, he wiggled his fingers and toes, and then flexed his arms and legs. He heard a cough and felt Billy moving around in his own bag.

Fort stretched out of his curled position and groped in the darkness around him. He squirmed his arms and shoulders out of the soft nylon sleeping bag and felt the drenched canvas of the tent cling to his skin.

He gasped for air and then flailed his arms, opening a space around his head. Within seconds he had the collapsed tent spread out enough so he could kneel. The wet canvas pressed down heavily on the back of his head and neck. His flashlight was digging into his shin. He forced himself to take slow, shallow breaths as he fought a rising sense of panic. The air reeked of vomit.

He switched on the flashlight and saw a huddled lump in a soggy sleeping bag. "Billy, are you all right?"

Fort heard a muffled, unintelligible reply, and then helped the boy find his way out of the bag. Fighting to control his own emotions, he searched the tent. He slipped into his soaked gray-and-brown pants and a sleeveless white-cotton undershirt before tugging on his hiking boots and baseball cap. Patting the big, baggy pockets on his pant-leg, he made sure he had his knife, compass, and a small first-aid kit.

"Come on, Billy, let's get out of here."

Fort didn't bother to look for the zipper of the tent door. With trembling fingers he found one of the jagged holes in the tent and ripped it wide open. He staggered to his feet and pushed the canvas aside.

Branches and twigs scratched him from all sides, and he realized they were in a thicket. He heard Billy crawl out of the tent, push the brush aside as he stood up, then whimper. Fort limped and clawed his way forward until he reached a clearing. The flashlight showed only the sprinkling rain and a few broken tree branches. No sign remained of the two adults or the five other boys. When Billy caught up to him, he turned the light off.

"What's wrong? Did the batteries die?" asked Billy.

"I'm letting my eyes get used to the darkness. Let's save the flashlight in case we really need it later."

Within seconds, Fort could distinguish various shades and shapes in the darkness. The sky was deep gray, with no stars or moon visible, and the black silhouettes of tree trunks towered around them. The air was heavy with moisture and the smell of wet earth and vegetation. He held his breath, listening to the rumble of distant thunder.

Something rustled in the brush in front of them. Billy gasped and grabbed Fort's arm. Heart pounding, Fort flicked the flashlight on and swung it toward the sound. Two glowing, yellow eyes glared up at him. A sudden hiss, quickly followed by what sounded like jaws snapping, sent him staggering backwards. His heel caught in the brush; he plopped down in the mud, and Billy toppled down next to him.

Fort scrambled back up, ready to run. The flashlight caught the glowing eyes again. This time, he could see a large bird on the ground just a few feet in front of him—an owl nearly two feet tall. Fort stepped back. He knew that the eyes of animals would often reflect a brilliant glow from a bright light and had seen this happen dozens of times when car headlights lit up wildlife.

The big bird raised a wing and hissed again. Two pointed tufts of feathers on top of the creature's head identified it as a Great Horned Owl. Fort had never seen one before, but recognized it from nature cards the Scouts used. Awesome.

One of the owl's wings hung awkwardly out to the side. Fort leaned forward for a closer look. With its broken wing dragging, the bird hopped onto a stout log. Fort's heart ached for the proud bird.

"What happened to it?" asked Billy.

"Probably crashed into a tree during the storm."

"Maybe we can catch it," said Billy, "and take it to someone who can help it."

Billy stepped toward the bird. Its big, yellow eyes glowered as it hissed, its beak snapping the air. The owl's good wing flapped up toward Billy, but the broken one flopped helplessly.

Fort gasped, imagining the bird's pain. "Come on. Let's go," he said. "We're only causing it more pain as it tries to defend itself from us. Better to leave it alone."

Fort hoped the wing would heal and the bird would survive, but he figured it more likely the owl would starve or be killed by other predators. Maybe he could find the bird in the morning and catch it. He would ask his dad and Mr. Crawford. The thought of the adults reminded Fort that he still had not heard from them or the five other Scouts. He guided Billy away from the owl, leaving it to fend for itself in its natural environment—darkness.

Taking a deep breath, he used it to yell his brothers' names. After hearing nothing, he called again. "Timmy! Tommy!"

This time he heard a faint reply through the rain. Fort headed in the direction of the voices as Billy tagged along through the dark, dripping woods.

Something cracked in the distance. Probably a tree limb breaking, thought Fort. He scanned the trees and bushes with his flashlight. Another pop of breaking wood sounded closer. Then he heard a rhythmic pounding that made the wet ground rumble as it came toward him. Heavy footsteps, approaching rapidly.

"Dad?" he yelled.

A large, black beast crashed through the thicket and bounded toward them. A cow, he realized. Heart surging in his chest, Fort pivoted aside, nearly tripping over Billy.

A rock-hard body slammed into him, knocking both boys to the ground. As he lay there staring into the darkness, Fort could hear the animal galloping through the woods, racing farther and farther away.

Another tree limb cracked in the distance, this time behind him. Then branches began to snap like firecrackers. Shortly, another huge, black silhouette flashed past him, then another, and another. He figured the cattle must have been frightened by the storm.

His flashlight lay in the mud by his feet. It threw a thin shaft of light onto the leaf-strewn ground. Before Fort could pick it up, another cow approached, heading straight for him. He yelled and waved his arms frantically as he stepped in front of Billy. The beast snorted and lurched to the side. Black legs streaked through the beam of the flashlight, then disappeared.

More tree limbs cracked, like breaking bones, in the distance. The rumble of dozens of pounding hooves drew closer. A stampede!

Fort grabbed Billy by the collar and dragged him through the slippery mud. Too late, he remembered the flashlight. He couldn't see a thing as he pushed aside the brush around him. Suddenly, his face smashed into something solid. Tree bark, rough as asphalt pavement, tore at his forehead. Dazed, he slumped to the ground and pulled Billy close behind the tree as dozens of cattle thundered past them in the darkness.

He closed his eyes and held his breath. The noise trailed into the distance. Easing his hold on Billy and breathing more easily, he started to get up. Then he heard another sound—more footsteps, but lighter, and moving slowly. Fort froze.

Something is sneaking up on us, he thought. His imagination running wild, he peeked around the tree into the darkness. Now yards away, the flashlight still cast a shaft of light into the woods. The black silhouette of a head appeared at the edge of the light. Smaller than the other animals, it turned toward Fort.

He caught his breath. He wanted to run but couldn't move. His throat constricting and heart pounding, he watched the shadowy figure move nearer, close to the ground. He imagined the beast crouching before it would leap at him. Closing his eyes, he waited for it to pounce and tear them to bloody shreds.

Suddenly, the air was ripped by a high-pitched *moo* that resounded through the woods. The mournful wail echoed into the night, then disappeared. For a moment total silence fell. Then, in the distance, Fort heard another long, but lower-pitched *moo.*

The animal close to the boys bellowed an answer that made Fort cringe. He looked again toward the flashlight. A small Black Angus calf trotted through the patch of light, and then disappeared into darkness. Fort closed his eyes and gasped for breath. Slower calves left behind in the stampede, like the little one he saw, would have to call to their mothers across the prairie, then catch up to them. He scolded himself for being frightened.

"Fort," said Billy with a sniffle, "I want to go home."

Fort almost laughed, but realizing how scared Billy was, he pulled the boy closer to his side and squeezed his shoulder gently. "Sounds good to me. Let's find the others."

He pulled himself to his feet and hobbled toward the dim circle of light. As he picked up his flashlight and wiped away the mud, sprinkling raindrops tapped the trees and ground around him.

"Timmy! Tommy!" he yelled again. His broad shoulders drooping, he listened.

"Help!" a boy's voice shouted in the distance. "Over here!"

Fort's hiking boots sank into the mud with each step. Slogging forward through the wet grass, he and Billy zigzagged and high-stepped over the branches and debris that littered the ground. He felt scrapes and bruises all over his body. A lump on his forehead throbbed, and he could taste blood mixed with the rainwater that trickled down his face. Fort paused, tenderly pressing the lump on his forehead, and tried to recall hitting his head. Billy ran ahead.

After a moment, Fort trudged onward toward the young voices in the distance. By alternately yelling and listening, he located the crumpled canvas of a tent propped against the trunk of a huge tree. Billy must have joined the others, because Fort could see three boy-sized lumps in the collapsed tent.

"You guys okay in there?" Fort asked.

"We want to go home!" a young voice yelled.

Fort recognized the shrill voice his twin brothers shared. Even he couldn't tell one from another. Scanning the woods in all directions, he saw no sign of the two adults or the other three eleven-year-olds. He searched the rumpled pile of wet canvas with his flashlight without finding the zipper, and wondered how Billy got inside, then realized it must be on the other side of the tent.

Fort backtracked and started to circle the crumpled pile of nylon. In the dim glow at the edge of the area lit by his flashlight, he could see a dark, corkscrew shape dangling from a tree like a huge jungle snake—an anaconda or a boa constrictor. Instinctively Fort stepped back, but the snake was already slipping across his neck!

Yelling and arms thrashing, he tried to swat the

serpent away. Instead, he felt himself entangled in moist, scaly coils. He swung his flashlight like a club as the snake wrapped itself around him. The light arced through the darkness in a crazy pattern as he thrashed at the reptile.

The snake slithered across his neck. He thrust it away and jumped to the side. His feet caught on something, and he stumbled into a writhing mass of serpent. Arms windmilling, legs kicking, Fort wrestled the rough-scaled body as it twisted on the ground. He screamed like a trapped animal as he imagined being crushed and swallowed, as in the nature shows on TV.

"Fort!" yelled one of his brothers. "What's going on out there?"

Wishing he had a hunting knife to stab into the snake's brain, Fort rolled and grabbed a stout section of the serpent's body. Clutching it tightly with one hand, he swung the flashlight in the other hand.

The flashlight hit the snake's body, but instead of the sound of flesh being pounded, Fort heard a *thunk* and a rattle that didn't sound right. He squinted closely at the serpent he was wrestling, but saw only twisted, bark-covered wood.

Fort released the wood in his hands and scooted to his knees, searching for the serpent that had attacked him. His senses fully alert, he stood ready to defend himself again, if necessary. Instead of a huge python, all Fort found was a very thick, looping vine. Still wary, he reached out and poked it. The moist, moss-covered bark felt exactly like the rough-scaled serpent he had just wrestled with.

As he turned in a circle, the beam of the flashlight lit ribbons of two-inch thick vine all around him. A section of the springy coil seemed to be suspended in mid-air. Fort aimed his light upward until he could see where a loop hung from the stub of a large tree branch.

Fort collapsed in the mud, a feeling of relief washing over him like a refreshing shower. His breathing and heart rate slowed, and he chuckled at himself for having imagined a killer snake where only a corkscrewing vine threatened him.

He recalled seeing pipe vines on numerous campouts. The woody vines were a common sight along creeks as they lay across the ground or twisted up the trunks of tall trees. Fort knew that anacondas and boa constrictors didn't live in Kansas, at least not in the wild. He peered at his surroundings again. The dark woods seemed determined to get him.

Fort felt a warm wetness that trickled down the inside of one thigh. In horrified disbelief, he realized that he had wet himself in fear during the "attack." He grabbed his pant leg, pulling the material away from his skin. For a moment, he was overcome by shame that screamed at him until he felt as if his head would explode. He wondered if he should take his pants off and let the rain rinse them. He would be mortified if anyone found out. His face warmed and felt steamy as raindrops sprinkled him.

"Fort, what are you doing out there?" a squeaky voice demanded. "We want to go home!"

Fort grit his teeth. Timmy and Tommy were always scolding him. Their voices grated on him like fingernails scratching a chalkboard. His face grew hot. What if his teasing, lazy, annoying little brothers found out he'd had the piss scared out of him by a pipe vine?

"Fort!" yelled a shrill voice from the tent.

Fort felt blood rush to his head, and his vision blurred. He knew what he was about to do. He hated himself for it, but he couldn't stop.

Growling, he picked up a thick stick, swung it in an arc over his head, and hammered it down on a boy-sized lump in the tent. A scream of pain and outrage erupted from his target. Another boy-sized lump in the canvas moved, and Fort swung the stick again.

The tent seemed alive with motion as confused and angry voices wailed and cried. In a frenzy, Fort continued to pound the tent, following the scrambling bodies as they moved under the canvas, and ignoring the screams.

Finally, he stopped, panting, and stared at the collapsed tent. He heard the boys groaning and sobbing, and glanced at the club in his hands. Teeth clenched, he slammed the ground with the stick until it shattered, and then hurled the broken stub into the darkness.

He felt numb. It had happened again. His temper had gone off like a bomb. A horrible sense of dread swept through him. What if he had really hurt someone this time? What if he had crippled or killed one of the boys? Kneeling at the edge of the collapsed tent, he grabbed a handful of wet nylon and pulled gently. The boys inside screamed.

"Hey, guys. I'm sorry," he said, even though he knew an apology wouldn't be nearly enough this time. "I'm going to pull on the tent until I can see the door. Okay?" Feeling and hearing the boys scramble and roll inside the tent, he lifted the wet canvas. He tugged again and again, until he could see the door, then zipped the tent flap open and crawled inside.

By flashlight he could see Billy and two cowering, wet boys, dressed only in their underwear. The tent, heavy with water, was draped over their heads and shoulders. Fort shined the flashlight on the freckled face of a red-haired boy. From the dimple on the boy's chin, he knew it was Tommy.

The boy glared at Fort, then attacked, fists pummeling Fort's face and head.

Fort's first reaction was to defend himself and fight back. Instead, he kept his arms at his sides, letting the smaller boy punish him. Tommy's attack slowed, then stopped. The boy crawled away from Fort, sobbing.

Before Fort could respond, Timmy was screaming at him. "Are you crazy? Why'd you hit us? We didn't do anything to you!"

Fort didn't have to look at Timmy to know the boy was crying from both pain and rage. Fort choked back his own tears. He never meant to hurt his little brothers or anyone else. He knew it wasn't their fault. His own temper was the problem.

He moved the flashlight to the third boy. Billy squinted, raised an arm to shield his eyes, then howled in agony. The thin, fair-haired boy cradled his left arm, his left hand twisted at a grotesque angle, his wrist broken.

CHAPTER THREE

Fort felt as if his insides would rip apart. He wanted to run away and never come back. Billy started to cry. Tommy and Timmy moved closer and stared wide-eyed at the little boy's arm.

"Billy," said Fort, "your arm hurts because it's broken. I'm really sorry. I'll go find Mr. Crawford and my dad. They'll know what to do." He turned to crawl out of the collapsed tent.

"Fort!" said Timmy. "You know first aid. You can help Billy."

Fort paused. Except for treating minor pocketknife wounds to himself, he had never had to provide first aid to anyone. He wished the adults were here, or even the older boys who had taught him first aid when he was a new Scout.

"I'll go get Dad," he repeated.

"Don't you dare leave us!" Tommy said. "Billy needs help right now."

"Please," said Timmy. "You can do it. I know you can."

Fort almost responded with a sarcastic remark, but

the expressions on his little brothers' faces stopped him. He could see the pain and disappointment in their eyes. A tingle zipped down his back. He shivered, blinked back tears, and took a deep breath as he thought about what to do next.

"Timmy and Tommy," he said, "I'll need two neckerchiefs and a long-sleeved shirt. Billy, sit still. I'll be right back."

A few minutes later, he crawled back into the collapsed tent with an armload of sticks. He forced several of the longer ones between the folds of canvas to hold the roof up as the rain intensified outside. Turning his attention back to the injured boy, he tried to remember his first-aid training.

"Billy, I'm sure it hurts a lot, but you're going to be fine," Fort said. "Can you be brave while I put on a splint? It'll make you more comfortable."

The frail, blond boy nodded and sniffed, tears still flowing.

"I'm not going to straighten your arm," said Fort, "because that would hurt a lot, and I don't want to cause more damage. I'll just put splints on. Don't worry, okay?"

Fort placed a short, thick stick on the front and one on the back of Billy's arm. "Now, Timmy, hold the sticks while I tie them in place."

He carefully wrapped a neckerchief around each end of the sticks and tied a square knot to hold them in place. He draped the shirt around Billy's slender neck and tied the sleeves together to make a sling for the broken arm. Then he grabbed a sleeping bag, unzipped it, and felt inside. It was dry. He gently wrapped the big, fluffy bag around Billy's shoulders.

"You'll be okay, now, Billy," said Fort.

"Shhh!" said Timmy. "I hear something."

Fort hoped the sloshing footsteps outside belonged to his dad and Mr. Crawford. The tent flap opened, and a flashlight shined in. Three more eleven-year-old boys crawled into the already crowded tent.

All six of the younger boys began talking at once.

"Man, I thought we were going to die!"

"The wind blew our tent into a fence."

"I think we were flying in the air for a while."

"Billy's arm is broken. Fort put a splint on it."

"Is Billy going to be okay?"

"I'm freezing."

"What happened, Fort?"

"Were we in a tornado?"

"Fort, where's Mr. Crawford and your dad?"

"Can we go home now?"

"Quiet!" yelled Fort, his head throbbing with all the questions. He took a deep breath before answering.

"Yes," he said, "I'm pretty sure that was a tornado. Yes, Billy will be fine, but we need to get him to a doctor soon. Timmy and Tommy, you'll be warmer if you put some clothes on.

"I don't know where Dad and Mr. Crawford are. I'm surprised they aren't here already. I'm going to find them. You guys stay here." He crawled over a Scout and sidled on his knees toward the tent door.

"Wait, Fort," said Timmy. "Aren't you supposed to take a buddy?"

Fort cringed.

"Mr. Crawford said three buddies are safer than two," said Tommy.

Fort resisted the urge to grab each of his scolding brothers by their curly, bright-red hair. They were right, of course. Always take a buddy, in case you get in trouble. Three buddies are better, so one can stay with an injured Scout and two can go for help. Fort doubted, however, if any of these little squirts would be much use if he got in trouble.

"You three—Chip, Booger, Jonathan," said Fort. "You guys come with me." He looked at his brothers and could tell they wanted to go with him, too.

"Timmy and Tommy," he said, "I really need you guys to look after Billy. Keep him warm and dry. We'll come back for you as soon as we find the adults."

Fort stepped out of the tent into the muddy darkness. Thunder rumbled in the distance. One by one, three younger boys emerged from the collapsed tent and stood next to him in the gentle rain. Their flashlights probed the surrounding brush.

The three Scouts were only as high as Fort's chest. They had outgrown their baby fat, but hadn't developed the muscles that rippled across Fort's six-foot-two-inch frame. At age eleven he had been much bigger than these boys. As far back as he could remember, he had been big for his age.

A light turned toward Fort, blinding him. He grabbed the flashlight and yanked it away from a small hand. "Now listen, you little twerps," he said. "I don't have time to baby-sit. I can use your help, but you'll have to do what I say. No running off to explore on your own and no horsing around, okay?" He didn't wait for a reply. "Right now," he continued, "we need to find the adults. Just be quiet and listen for a minute."

Fort yelled for his dad, then waited, ears straining to hear a response. He knew the adults would get Billy to a doctor as soon as possible, but he dreaded telling his father and Mr. Crawford that he had broken Billy's arm. He was in real trouble this time—he might even have to go to jail.

"Fort, which way—"

"Quiet." Fort glared at Booger. "Help me listen." He yelled again, then gestured for silence. Nothing but distant thunder.

As he listened for the adults, he saw Booger hitch his hip to the side, then reach down to the crotch of his jeans and begin to scratch. Fort turned to the other boys. "Okay, I guess we're going to have to go find the adults."

"Come on, guys, let's go," said the thin, freckle-faced boy called Jonathan. The three younger boys started to walk into the woods.

Fort laughed. "Where do you think you're going? Do you have any idea where the adult camp is from here, or which direction you're walking?" By his flashlight Fort could see the boys stop and look at each other. Jonathan grinned sheepishly at Fort and shrugged.

Fort took a deep breath before continuing. "I remember that the wind was blowing from the southwest when the thunder woke me."

"How do you know that?" asked Timmy's best friend Chip. A bright, white picture of a NASA space shuttle filled the front of the short, round boy's tee shirt.

"Because the southwest corner of my tent was getting pounded by the wind," said Fort, hoping he was right. "So let's assume the storm blew all of us to the northeast." How far? he wondered. Fifty yards? A hundred? Two hundred? "We'll spread out a little and walk southwest from here. Let's find our campsite. Then we'll have a point of reference to find the adults' camp."

"But, Fort," asked Booger, "which way is southwest?"

Fort patted the lower-left pocket of his gray-and-brown camouflage pants, unsnapped the flap, and pulled out his compass. He twisted the compass housing so the direction-of-travel arrow pointed to 225 degrees, indicating southwest, and held the compass level in front of him, waist high. With the flashlight he could see the red needle sway gently inside the liquid-filled compass, then nearly stop. He turned his body until the red needle pointed to "N" on the compass housing.

"That way." He pointed toward the southwest. "And spread out," he added. "Keep your eyes open so we don't walk right past our campsite."

Fort estimated they had hiked about a hundred yards when the younger Scouts started to chatter.

"I see a backpack," a young voice yelled.

"Here's our campfire," said another boy.

They all gathered at the rocks that had formed a ring around their campfire that evening.

"Hey," said Chip, "where's the rest of our stuff?"

A cast-iron frying pan lay in the mud. Everything else was gone. Fort's concern for his father and Mr. Crawford increased as he considered their next move.

"The adult camp was about fifty yards north of ours," he said, then checked the compass again and hurried in that direction. The boys caught up quickly and spread out on either side of him.

Soon their flashlights shined on the remains of the adult campsite. The tent and the backpacks were gone, leaving just a soggy pit of black coals. Fort noticed that the trees in the area were even more damaged than at the boys' campsite. His fingers trembled as he reset his compass for northeast. "Spread out!" he yelled. "Go that way!"

Searching with flashlights, they scrambled through an obstacle course of fallen tree limbs.

"I see a backpack!" shouted Jonathan. "I think it's Mr. Crawford's."

They searched the area more closely and then trudged farther into the darkness. Soon they came to the edge of the creek, and Fort shined his flashlight across the water.

"Look!" yelled Chip.

One of the flashlights cast a pool of light around a dark object at the water's edge—a half-submerged tent. Fort broke into a run.

"Dad!" he shouted. "Mr. Crawford!"

A corner of the tent protruded from the creek. Fort grabbed it and pulled. "Guys! Help me get this out of the water."

They all tugged as hard as they could. The tent wouldn't budge.

"Hold it!" Fort slipped his knife from his pocket, then slashed through the tent fabric until the blade stopped at a seam.

He stuck his arm through the gaping hole in the tent and fished around until he could feel water-soaked cloth. Yanking it out, he recognized it as his father's red Scout jacket. Fort tossed the jacket aside and thrust his arm and shoulder deep into the partially submerged tent. His fingers brushed against clammy, wet flesh.

He jerked his hand back, his skin crawling.

"Dad!" He plunged his arm back into the hole, grabbed a cold, wet wrist, and pulled it up and out of the tent.

"Hurry!" he yelled at the younger boys. "Help me get him out!"

The eleven-year-olds had frozen at the sight of the arm extending from the tent.

"Grab and pull," Fort ordered. "Now!"

The boys hurried forward and helped Fort wrestle the man out of the tent. They dragged the body up the slippery bank of the creek.

Fort rolled the man over on his back. By flashlight, he could see a silvery-gray beard—Mr. Crawford. The man's head had flopped to the side. His neck was broken. Fort shuddered, knowing the Scoutmaster was dead. Still, he placed his trembling fingers on the side of his neck, just over the carotid artery. The skin was cold and lifeless. He felt no pulse.

A small hand tapped Fort's shoulder. "What's that sound?" Jonathan asked.

Fort pointed his flashlight toward the creek. The water was a lot higher than it had been only minutes earlier, and it was flowing faster and louder.

"Move uphill, now!" yelled Fort. "You guys take Mr. Crawford. I'll get Dad."

Fort hurried back to the partly submerged tent. He reached in and pulled out a pile of wet clothes, then tossed them aside and plunged back into the tent. His hand touched a man's head. Fort grabbed a handful of hair and pulled until he could slip his hands under his father's arms, then lifted and hauled him backward out of the tent.

His dad's heels made tracks in the mud as Fort scrambled up the bank. One of Fort's feet slid out from under him, and he fell onto his rear end, nearly pulling his dad on top of him. Rising water sloshed and gurgled at his feet. He heard the younger boys screaming at each other as they struggled to drag Mr. Crawford's body up the hill.

Fort stood and pulled his father upright. He bent and draped his dad's body over one shoulder like a football practice dummy, then staggered uphill until they were well above the rising water. The younger boys had gathered next to a thicket. Fort carried his father into the brush and eased him down on the ground next to Mr. Crawford.

Fort knelt and lowered his ear to his father's mouth. He couldn't hear a breath and didn't see a rise or fall in his dad's chest. No pulse, either.

Fort's heart raced as he tried to remember CPR. He had received training from several different instructors over the years, but now the specific steps were a jumbled blur in his mind. Where should he start? Then he remembered one instructor saying, "Cardiopulmonary Resuscitation, CPR, is as simple as ABC."

"'A' is for air—clear the air passage," Fort said aloud. Tilting his father's head back, he pushed the lower jaw down with his thumb and listened for breathing again. Nothing. He shined his flashlight into his dad's mouth. He couldn't see anything blocking the throat. The flesh inside his father's mouth was not just wet, but also warm. Maybe there's still hope.

"'B' is for breathing," he recited. He took in a lungful of air, put his mouth over his dad's open mouth, and blew out a strong breath. Warm, moist air feathered across Fort's cheek, coming from his father's nose. Grumbling at his oversight, he gently pinched his father's nostrils together and blew another breath into his dad's mouth. This time he could see his father's chest rise as air filled the lungs.

Fort drew back and let the body exhale on its own. Again, he fitted his mouth over his father's, inflated his dad's lungs, then let the body exhale by itself. He rechecked for a pulse. Nothing.

"'C' is for circulation," he continued. He repositioned himself so he was straddling his dad's waist. He placed his hand, palm down, on his father's chest, 'right between the nipples,' he remembered. He placed the palm of his other hand over the first one and interlocked his fingers. Straightening his arms and locking his elbows, he thrust down firmly on his father's chest.

Fort pushed harder and harder until he could hear and feel the cartilage in his father's chest crack. He cringed at the sound, but kept going. After fifteen thrusts he stopped and returned to his position for rescue breathing.

Fort repeated the cycle of two breaths and fifteen chest thrusts several times. He tried to remember if CPR could actually restart a heart. At best, it was probably a slim possibility without expert help and the right equipment. Closing his eyes, he prayed for help.

He could feel himself getting tired and wondered how long he could continue. He would have to pace himself to conserve his own strength, but knew he wouldn't give up as long as there was any hope of reviving his dad.

After another cycle, Fort could feel a faint pulse in the carotid artery. With tears in his eyes, he continued the rescue breathing. He no longer needed to thrust down on the chest, because his father's heart was pumping by itself. "Even a weak heartbeat will pump more blood than the CPR chest thrust," he recalled an instructor saying.

Just as Fort had finished blowing another lung full of air, his father coughed violently, followed by a deep, rasping breath. Again came a wrenching cough. His dad's eyes open as he gasped for another breath. After he gave a series of violent coughs and wheezing breaths, his eyes closed, and he settled into peaceful, sleeplike breathing.

Exhausted, Fort slumped in the mud next to his father. Raindrops mixed with the tears pouring down his cheeks. Excited young voices caused Fort to turn. Timmy, Tommy, and Billy approached.

"We had to leave the tent," said Tommy, panting. "It flooded and washed away. We heard voices, so we came this way." He spotted the bodies of the adults, and his voice quavered. "What's wrong?"

CHAPTER FOUR

Fort sat quietly as the overcast sky brightened. During the night he and the other Scouts had collected as much of their camping gear as they could find by flashlight. A shredded tent, now draped over the thicket, had provided some shelter from the rain. His unconscious father lay wrapped in a sleeping bag. He had covered Mr. Crawford's body with a dark-blue plastic tarp that the Scouts had used for a ground cover. The younger boys were a sleeping jumble of bodies sprawled across the grass, mud, and various pieces of clothing.

Ashamed that he had broken Billy's arm in a fit of rage, Fort knew that his humiliation from imagining a python in the dark, or even from wetting his pants, was not a valid excuse. He tugged at his pant leg and squirmed, thankful that the ongoing rain had rinsed him clean.

He was pretty sure that Mr. Crawford had been dead when they had pulled him out of the tent, but wondered if he should have given the Scoutmaster CPR anyway. Would others blame him for Mr.

Crawford's death? Had he been right to leave Mr. Crawford to search for his own father? The questions nagged at him, even though he thought he had done all he could.

Shivering, he leaned over his father and listened to shallow breathing. Fort wondered what else he should do, as he brushed wet hair back from his dad's forehead—curly red hair, like Timmy's and Tommy's, not the straight, dark-brown hair Fort shared with his mother. He placed his hand on his dad's forehead, as his mom always did when Fort was sick. No fever.

"Dad, can you hear me?" He patted his father's freckled cheeks, hoping his eyelids would flutter open. He worried that his father might never wake up—or never be quite the same. He might have been without oxygen for a long time. Fort's heart ached to think of life without his dad.

From the corner of his eye, he noticed movement in the tall weeds a few yards away. A doglike face stared at him with serious brown eyes. At first he thought it was a stray mutt, then recognized it as a coyote. Fort felt his pulse quicken and his insides jitter. The coyote's yellowish-brown head turned as its ears pointed forward. A drooling tongue dangled to the side between its pointed yellow teeth as the animal panted.

Fort tried to remember if coyotes ever attacked

humans. He had always heard that they were cowardly, avoiding people as much as possible. The brush behind the animal rustled. Another coyote stepped closer and then crouched low to the ground, almost disappearing into the vegetation. With growing concern, Fort scanned the thicket carefully, spotting a patch of scraggly hair in one place and a raggedy pointed ear in another, until he counted four more coyotes.

Fort felt himself panicking. A lone coyote was one thing. Six was another. Surely they wouldn't attack him and the boys. Coyotes were known for their cunning and stealth, surviving on rabbits and mice and whatever carrion was available. Then it dawned on him: the coyotes weren't after Fort and the boys. They must have picked up the scent of Mr. Crawford's corpse. Fort glanced toward the blue tarp next to his dad, assuring himself that the body was undisturbed.

He wondered if the coyotes were desperate enough to attack. Then he remembered that coyotes were also called prairie wolves, and he was facing a whole pack of them. In his mind, Fort saw the beasts rushing forward like wolves, overpowering him, and savagely tearing at the human bodies.

His blood seemed to boil within him. He needed a weapon, something more substantial than the knife in his pocket. Seeing an outcropping of loose rocks a short distance away, Fort sprang to his feet and ran. As he dashed toward the outcropping, he heard movements in the brush behind him and imagined the tawny demons racing after him. He would feel their razor-sharp teeth any moment now. If he tripped, they would be all over him.

Reaching the outcropping, Fort snatched up a rock and spun around. He drew his hand back, ready to mash in the head of the first coyote to reach him. He paused, confused. No prairie wolves were rushing him. In fact, he couldn't see any coyotes at all. They must have gone directly to Mr. Crawford's body.

Fort rushed back to the thicket, dreading what he might see there. But the boys were still sleeping in a pile, his dad was still unconscious, and the blue tarp appeared to be undisturbed. He searched the brush around the thicket until he was satisfied that the coyotes were gone, and then grimaced with relief. The skittish animals had probably sped in the opposite direction while he had run toward the outcropping of rocks. They're probably a mile away by now, he thought, a little embarrassed.

As Fort eased himself down next to his dad, he became aware of the effects of the disastrous morning. His eyes felt scratchy and tight from lack of sleep. His whole body ached. He was physically and mentally exhausted, hungry and thirsty. He grieved for Mr. Crawford and feared for his father's life. Whether he liked it or not, he was responsible for six eleven-year-old Boy Scouts, including one with a broken arm.

Originally, they had camped among trees that formed a canopy above a creek that wound its way across the prairie. Now bare stumps surrounded them. Huge clumps of roots and dirt were exposed where stately trees had once stood. Everywhere, broken-and-mangled tree limbs littered the ground. The scene reminded Fort of bombed-out jungles in old war movies.

Mr. Crawford's burgundy-colored minivan lay on its side, its roof crushed against the trunk of a giant cottonwood tree. The tree itself was limbless, a thirty-foot-high post. The roof of his father's blue Blazer was only partly visible. Another tree trunk, nearly two feet thick, had crushed the front end of the vehicle. Fort realized the boys were lucky to be alive.

He had already decided that his first job of the morning would be to start a fire: flames to warm them and lift their spirits, smoke to alert potential rescuers of the group's location, and heat to cook a hot meal—if they could find food.

Fort hobbled to a nearby cedar tree that had

somehow survived the storm and gingerly pushed between its prickly limbs. He welcomed the clean, sweet smell of evergreen. As he had hoped, the cedar was nearly dry under its canopy of needles. He cut off small, dead branches until he had an armload of twigs, branches, and brown needles.

He selected a bare patch of ground and sorted through the pile, accumulating handfuls of dead cedar needles for tinder. On top of the prickly needles, Fort piled toothpick-sized twigs for kindling, then small branches, and finally the largest of the limbs.

The boys had recovered Fort's backpack during the night. Unzipping a muddy side pouch, he fished out the brown-plastic medicine bottle that contained his wooden matches. He glanced around, looking for something rough and dry enough to strike the match, but everything he saw was still damp.

He flicked the white tip of the red match head with his thumbnail. Part of the tip crumbled and fell, and he grumbled to himself. When he had been a new Scout, he had often needed a dozen matches to light a campfire. Now he took pride in his skill at starting a fire with just one. Licking his lips, he concentrated and tried again. This time the match flashed, and then ignited.

Sheltering the flame with cupped hands, he

lowered it to the dead cedar needles. The prickly needles quickly caught fire, and the flames stretched upward into the dry twigs. The kindling crackled and produced larger flames, which licked at the branches on top. Soon he had a sizable blaze.

Fort dragged a log next to the fire and sat down. The smoke and the crackle of burning wood soon roused the younger Scouts. Within minutes all of the boys had huddled around the fire with Fort. For a while they all quietly warmed themselves and yawned.

Jonathan was the first to speak. "I'm hungry."

This was followed by a chorus of, "Me, too."

"Fort, my arm hurts." Billy cradled his arm.

"Is Dad in a coma?" asked Timmy.

"I want to go home," said Chip, who then burst into tears.

One by one, each of the other boys began to sob. Fort fought back his own tears. His throat tightened, and he shifted his position on the log just as one of the other boys stood up. The log rolled forward, and Fort toppled backwards into the mud. The boys hooted in laughter.

Blood rushed to Fort's head, and his vision blurred. "You crybabies make me sick!" he shouted. "I can't wait to get rid of you!"

Before he could stop himself, he lunged toward the

younger boys. Timmy toppled backwards off the log. Fort straddled him, fist raised. Suddenly, Tommy jumped in front of him and grabbed his wrist.

"Stop it!" yelled Tommy. "Before you hurt somebody—again."

Fort hesitated. He glared at Tommy and looked down at Timmy. Seeing the fear and hurt in his little brother's eyes, he sank back onto the log, then leaned forward and covered his face with his hands.

After a moment, he looked up and stared blankly in the direction of the thicket where the blue tarp covering the Scoutmaster's body showed through the brush. He recalled a conversation they had had several months earlier.

"Learning to control your emotions is part of growing up," Mr. Crawford had told him. "Our ability to control our behavior is one of the things that separates humans from other animals. That doesn't mean you always hide your emotions. There are times when strong emotions are necessary. Even anger. But Fort, you can't let your temper—especially yours—get out of control."

"I've tried, Mr. Crawford," Fort had said, "but it just boils over and I can't stop until it's too late."

The Scoutmaster had looked him in the eye before responding. "The fact that you recognize the problem shows that you're maturing. Now you need to do something about it, before you really hurt somebody and mess up your own life in the process."

Their conversation had been cut short when another Scout had interrupted them.

Fort stared at the blue tarp covering Mr. Crawford's body. He felt an emptiness in his chest and knew he would miss his old friend. All they could do for him now was to protect his body until his family could bury him.

Hearing a cough, Fort turned. The six younger boys were staring at him. He recognized the expressions on their faces and sighed. Even though he had hurt Billy and scared them all again this morning, they still looked up to him, expecting him to know what to do. He stood up and leaned over the fire to warm his hands.

"Can we go home now?" asked Booger in a voice muffled by his finger probing the depths of his nose.

Fort cleared his throat before answering. "Guys, I'm afraid we're stuck here for a while."

"Maybe we can get the cars to start," said freckle-faced Jonathan. "I'll drive."

"You idiot," said Chip. "You don't know how to drive."

"I do, too," said Jonathan. "At least better than

you."

Timmy stood up and pointed to the vehicles. "Get real, guys. The van and the Blazer are wrecked."

Fort didn't say anything. He was pretty sure they wouldn't get far in the mud, even if one of the vehicles could be started.

"Okay, then," said Jonathan, "let's just hike back to the ranch house. Then we can call home, and our parents will come and get us."

Several of the boys agreed and stood up as if they were ready to go.

"Wait a minute," said Fort. "Dad might have internal injuries. He shouldn't be moved, and Billy shouldn't move either, with his broken arm."

At the mention of his name, Billy started to cry. He held the injured arm as he rocked back and forth on the log he shared with the others. "Fort, it really hurts!"

Guilt and shame slicing deep through him, Fort knelt in the mud in front of the thin boy. Peeking under the makeshift splint, he was relieved to see that the hand had somehow straightened itself out and was no longer at an unnatural angle to the arm. "Billy, I'm really sorry. It's my fault. I lost my temper. We'll get you to a doctor as soon as possible."

Billy continued to sob, and Fort put his hand on the boy's shoulder. "What does your mom give you for pain at home? Do you remember what it's called?"

The boy blinked a couple of times, and then gave the brand name of a popular painkiller.

Fort pulled a small plastic bottle from his backpack. "Is this what your mom gives you?"

The blond-haired boy nodded.

Relieved that the boy wasn't allergic to the medicine, Fort opened the bottle and gave Billy two tablets. One of the other boys handed Billy a canteen of water. Fort ruffled the boy's soft hair. "You're going to be okay." Nevertheless, he felt a rising sense of desperation. He knew Billy needed medical attention as soon as possible.

"Is Dad going to die, too?" asked Timmy.

The question jolted Fort. Seeing the worried look on both of his little brothers' faces, he felt his throat tighten and his lips tremble. He couldn't answer the question.

"Is he in a coma, or just sleeping?" asked Chip.

Fort shrugged, not knowing how to tell the difference.

"If he's in a coma," said Chip, "we should talk to him anyway. It might help him wake up sooner. I saw that on TV once."

"So, what are we going to do?" asked Jonathan. "I mean, if we can't drive out, and we aren't going to walk out, are we going to just sit here and wait?"

"Well, my mom and your parents know where we are," said Fort. "If they know a tornado came anywhere near us, they'll come out to check. Even if they don't know about the tornado, they'll come looking for us when we don't show up at home this afternoon. Besides, the ranch house is only a few miles away, so maybe Mrs. Newton and Tana will find us. Either way, we're on our own for at least a few more hours."

"We're just going to sit here until somebody finds us?" asked Jonathan.

"Besides taking care of Dad and Billy, there are several things we should do," answered Fort. "Let's keep a big fire burning and make as much smoke as possible. Let's make a big 'X' out of rocks and wood. I have a small mirror in my pack. Maybe we can flash sunlight at an airplane. The smoke, the reflected light, and the big 'X' are all signals that might get someone's attention and bring help sooner."

"Can I flash the mirror at the airplanes?" asked Billy, as he wiped the last of his tears on a sleeve.

"Sure," Fort said, relieved that Billy seemed to be feeling better. "Who wants to make the big 'X' on the ground over there in that little meadow?"

Chip and Timmy volunteered.

"Jonathan and Booger, would you gather as much of the camping equipment as you can find?" asked Fort. "Tommy, would you keep an eye on Dad, talk to him, and gather a pile of firewood?"

Fort paused and looked around. "I'll search the cars for anything useful."

As he approached his father's dark-blue Blazer, he could see that both the windshield and hood were crushed. The door handle on the driver's side wouldn't budge, even when he yanked on it with all his strength. He stepped to the rear of the vehicle and pushed the button on the rear hatch. It popped open.

The cargo area behind the seats was strewn with the kind of miscellaneous items his dad usually took on campouts. He often stored extra food in the car to keep it away from night-prowling raccoons. Fort spotted a cooler and pulled the top off. Inside were a carton of eggs and packages of sausage, tortillas, and vegetables. He lifted the cooler out of the Blazer and set it on the ground. Then he climbed inside and rummaged through the gear, tossing to the ground items that might be useful.

He noticed the key in the ignition, so he squeezed between the front seats, brushed aside broken bits of windshield glass, and slipped behind the steering wheel. Not really expecting the car to start, he turned the key anyway. A grinding noise came from under the hood, followed by a loud bang. Fort released the ignition key, and the engine noise stopped. A twangy, country-western tune blared from the radio. Fort frowned. He and his father had different tastes in music.

Resting his forehead on the steering wheel, he listened as the old tune played on the radio. Something about a poker game—knowing when to hold the cards and when to fold them. Right now, thought Fort, I'd be happy to fold 'em.

A radio announcer cut into the song. "Now for a special news update from Bob Walters, live from Strickler, Kansas."

Fort sat upright—Strickler was their hometown.

Another male voice came across the speaker. "As we reported earlier, a tornado struck this peaceful southeast Kansas community late last night. Predawn reports indicated severe damage to the town."

"It's obvious now," continued the reporter, "that the damage is much worse than originally thought. I'm standing on a hillside road just north of Strickler. The city looks as if it were bombed flat last night. The buildings that didn't get blown away are piles of rubble. This is the worst tornado damage I've seen in over twenty years as a reporter. The governor has been asked to send National Guard troops to help search for victims and to clear the streets for emergency vehicles.

"Twenty-six deaths have been reported so far, and dozens of injuries. Those numbers are likely to get much higher as more buildings are searched. The sheriff has not yet released the names of those killed last night, because relatives have not yet been notified. I'm afraid the damage here is so bad that it may take days to search damaged buildings and to clear . . ."

Fort felt himself getting dizzy as his hands shook, and tears streamed from his eyes. His mother was at home in Strickler. She could be dead, in a hospital, or trapped under a collapsed building, and he couldn't get home to help her.

After a few minutes he climbed out of the car, lifted the plastic cooler of food, and trudged toward the campsite. He could see the boys adding wood to the fire, and he could hear their chatter.

Fort's eyes still stung from tears, and he took a deep breath. He had to decide whether or not to tell these boys that their hometown had been devastated by the tornado. Their families and homes might have been wiped out.

He also realized that their own situation was now much more difficult. They could no longer rely on their families to rescue them. Their families, if they were still alive, were fighting their own battles, unaware that the Scouts were also in trouble. He and the boys were on their own.

CHAPTER
FIVE

Fort helped the boys fix breakfast over the campfire. They cooked sausages and scrambled eggs in a cast-iron skillet, then wrapped the sausages and eggs in tortillas to make breakfast burritos. They warmed Pop-Tarts and heated water from their canteens to make hot chocolate. The familiar routine of camp cooking calmed Fort as he thought about what to do next.

He considered telling the younger Scouts about the tornado damage, but knew the news would scare them and make them worry about their families. They could do nothing about their families at this point anyway, so he decided the boys didn't need to know the situation at home.

A soft, but persistent thumping sound caught his attention. Turning to the younger boys, he half expected to see one of them drumming on a log. As the noise grew louder, he dropped the pan he was holding and raced into the little meadow. The thumping sound grew to a deafening *whomp-whomp-whomp* that seemed to come from right above their camp.

Suddenly, the sky above the mangled treetops was filled with three huge, fast-moving helicopters. Fort's joy was replaced by fear as the sound increased to a level that hammered the air around him, reverberating through his body and pounding the ground under his boots. As quickly as the green army choppers had appeared, they passed over him and moved onward. He screamed and waved his arms over his head as he jumped up and down.

He waved and shouted until his throat felt hoarse. But the helicopters flew steadily in an easterly direction until they shrunk to little dots in the sky, and the *whomp-whomp-whomp* of their rotors diminished to a soft thumping sound once again. For the first time Fort realized that the younger boys had been yelling and waving beside him. After the helicopters disappeared over the horizon, all fell silent.

"Why didn't they stop?" said Billy, sniffling.

Fort started to answer, but his throat suddenly felt tight. He coughed and shook his head. Turning away so the boys wouldn't see the moisture in his own eyes, he signaled them to follow him back to the camp.

They all moped around the fire for a few minutes. Fort had seen military helicopters on many previous occasions as they crisscrossed Kansas, usually flying to and from Fort Riley in the north-central part of the state. This morning they were probably heading for Strickler to help tornado victims.

Fort looked toward his father lying unconscious in the thicket, then at Billy with his broken arm. The helicopters had been the big kind that could have easily carried all of them out in one trip.

"Why didn't they see our fire and our big 'X'?" asked Jimmy.

"I tried to flash the mirror," said Billy, "but the sun wasn't shining."

Fort shrugged. "They were flying low and pretty fast. I guess they just didn't notice." The helicopter crew would have had a better chance of seeing them if the choppers had been higher and farther away, he reasoned. They had probably been flying low to keep under the cloud cover. "Just bad luck, guys."

They all sat quietly. Fort tried to shake off his disappointment and think about what they should do next.

"All right, here's the plan," he said, in a voice that sounded more confident than he actually felt. "Timmy and Chip will stay here with Billy and Dad. Your job is to look after Dad and to keep the fire burning and smoking. Billy, you keep an eye on the sky and be ready to flash the mirror. Maybe we'll get lucky and someone will see you."

"But, Fort," asked Timmy, "where are you guys going?"

Fort paused before answering. "The rest of us are going back to the ranch house. Mrs. Newton will be able to get help for us. We'll come back for you as soon as we can."

"Don't leave us," wailed Timmy. "Why don't you let the others go, and you stay here with us?"

"We don't know what to do," said Chip.

"I'm scared," Billy said, "and my arm really hurts."

Fort could see the fear in their faces and wished he had a better solution to their problem. He had decided that Timmy was the boy he most trusted to leave with his dad and Billy, and that Chip would have trouble keeping up on a long hike anyway.

"Listen," he said. "It's several miles back to the ranch house, across a mixture of scrub brush and open pasture. I don't feel comfortable sending you guys out by yourselves. Too many things can go wrong. So I have to go. I'll go with three buddies, to be safe, just as you said."

Billy started to whimper and sniffle as Fort borrowed Timmy's daypack and placed his water bottles and first-aid kit inside. Fearing that the bottles would roll around inside the little pack, Fort pulled a tee shirt from his backpack and stuffed it into the smaller daypack.

"We're stuck here until we get help," Fort continued calmly, "and help probably won't come unless we bring it here. Otherwise, it could be days before somebody finds us."

He looked from face to face. "You guys decide. We'll do it democratically. The choice is between going for help now, or just waiting and hoping we don't have to spend another night out here. Okay? Raise your hand if you want to risk spending another night away from home."

As Fort expected, no hands went up. Maybe his phrasing wasn't very democratic, but he wasn't in the mood for an argument.

"Okay, that settles it," he said. "Tommy, Booger, Jonathan, and I will hike back to the ranch house. The rest of you will stay with Dad, keep the fires going, and watch for airplanes. There's plenty of water and a big can of pork and beans in the back of the Blazer. You'll be fine." He saw the scared look on their faces. "I promise we'll get help as soon as possible." He swallowed hard, then added, "No matter what."

Fort and the three younger Scouts were soon slogging along a dirt road that wound between thickets of wild plum and dogwood. The road had been hard and dusty the previous day. Now, freshly soaked, the surface was sticky, dark-brown mud.

A new layer of muck accumulated on Fort's hiking boots with every step he took, until each boot felt as if it weighed twenty pounds. He carefully balanced each mud-laden foot as he moved it ahead and set it down. Leaning forward, he yanked the other foot out of the goo and then repeated the process.

He remembered hiking in the rain at the Philmont Scout Ranch in New Mexico. At least the mud there hadn't sucked at his feet like this. The soil in the mountains, he had discovered, was filled with sand and gravel. Here in this part of Kansas, the soil was heavy with clay that became nearly as hard as cement when dry, but was slippery muck when wet.

Fort kicked his foot forward, sending a huge blob of mud sailing in front of him. Encouraged, he kicked his other foot in the same way. Another blob tumbled ahead. His boots much lighter now, he continued to tramp. He imagined he was Bigfoot as he left huge tracks in the road. The extra effort was quickly wearing him out, and they hadn't even walked a quarter of a mile.

The younger Scouts were well ahead of Fort, and he could hear their chattering and giggling. They looked like goblins plodding down the road. Fort watched as Booger lost his balance in mid-step and toppled to the ground.

The boy rolled over, scooted up on his hands and knees, and then wobbled to a standing position. His face, chest, arms, and legs were dark with mud. Tommy and Jonathan hooted with laughter. Booger scraped a handful of mud off his face and hurled it at Tommy. Red-haired Tommy ducked the flying mud ball, then scooped his own mud off the road and flung it back at Booger. A three-way battle of flying mud missiles erupted with the boys shouting and laughing.

Fort tramped ahead to the boys. As he approached, they eyed him warily. This puzzled him until he realized that he himself was the cause of their concern. Shame flowed through him and twisted his insides until they ached.

Why wouldn't they fear me? Within the last twenty-four hours, I've punched one of my little brothers and broken Billy's arm. I nearly lost control again this morning. He ground his teeth silently as he realized for the first time that he had truly earned his nickname: The Brute.

He pointed to a pile of rocks beside the road and took a seat, noticing that the other boys sat several yards away, facing him. He unclipped the canteen from his belt and took a drink, then began scraping thick mud from his shoes. As he cleaned his boots, he casually studied the other boys.

His red-haired brother, sitting to the left, wore a purple ball cap with a stylized silver wildcat on the front: a Kansas State University power-cat. Lanky, auburn-haired, and freckled Jonathan sat in the middle, his tee shirt sporting the image of a black-hooded professional wrestling star. Round-faced, dark-haired Booger sat to the right, flipping something from the end of his middle finger.

Fort watched as Booger coughed slightly, his face contorting as if he were gagging. The boy inhaled and then hawked something into the air. Fort realized too late that the flying object was arcing toward him. He heard a splat and felt something hit his boot. Looking down, he cringed at the sight of a slimy blob of yellowish-gray phlegm oozing down the toe of his boot. His reaction was immediate—he was on his feet and moving toward Booger.

Tommy darted in front of him. "He didn't mean anything, Fort. Just calm down."

Fort felt pressure on his chest and looked down. Tommy pushed hard to hold him back. Fort stopped.

"Booger," Tommy commanded, "tell Fort you're sorry."

Fort could see that Booger had scrambled backwards to avoid him. Now the bushy-browed boy looked confused.

"Why?" he asked. "What'd I do?" He wiped his mouth and nose with a sleeveless arm. "And quit calling me Booger. My name is Roger."

Somebody giggled, and Fort realized that he had nearly lost his temper again. He backed off, wiping his boot clean in the damp grass at the side of the road.

"I'm getting tired," said Jonathan. "Isn't there a shortcut that isn't so muddy?"

Fort's attention returned to the road lined with thick brush. He considered their situation for a moment as the boys drank from their canteens. Then he pulled out his compass. "I'm guessing the ranch house is about three miles south and west of our camp. Let's leave the road and hike cross-country. The pasture should be easier to walk through than this slop."

Fort led the boys through a landscape of small trees, grass, and tall weeds that confined their view to the immediate area. His pant legs were soon wet from the damp grass, and he shivered in the cool morning air. It's better than slogging along the muddy road, he figured. Ahead, the younger boys climbed between the spiked strands of a barbed-wire fence, then wandered out into a pasture.

After checking his compass, Fort scaled the fence and set off after the boys. He was relieved to see fewer weeds and less brush on this side of the fence. Walking was much easier. His boot caught on something, and he stumbled. Looking back, he saw an upturned patty of dried cow manure.

Curious, he flipped the pie-sized cow chip over with the toe of his boot, and then picked it up. Although it was still a little damp on the outside from the rain, it seemed totally dry and surprisingly light, almost like cork. He recalled that pioneers crossing the treeless plains had used buffalo chips as fuel for their cook fires, then tried to imagine how those fires must have smelled.

He called to the jabbering boys many yards ahead, and when they stopped to look back at him, he tossed the piece of manure like a Frisbee. Not really expecting the chip to reach the boys, he was tickled to see it glide upward, then drift sideways toward them.

Jonathan shouted and raced toward the disk. He leaped and almost caught it before it coasted past him, then slammed into the ground.

Fort laughed as the exploding turd showered Tommy and Booger with dozens of fragments. The boys searched the ground around them. Then Tommy began laughing, too, as he picked a round, thick chip off the ground and hurled it in Fort's direction. It wobbled like a duck, then disintegrated in mid flight and fell harmlessly to the ground. Soon all three of the eleven-year-olds were shrieking and running ahead while searching for more chips to throw at each other.

Hurrying across the pasture after them, Fort slowed occasionally to kick cow chips, sending them flying or rolling ahead. He was eager to get to the ranch house—and not just to get help for his dad and Billy. Maybe he would see Tana Newton again. Plodding onward, he recalled their arrival at the ranch house on the previous day.

Mr. Crawford had eased his minivan around the Newton's large red barn and had parked in front of their old, white, two-story house. The bearded Scoutmaster had waited for Fort's dad to join him, and together they had walked to the screened porch. A middle-aged woman Fort didn't recognize greeted the two men at the door. Fort knew that Mr. Crawford liked to visit. They would probably chat a while before moving on to the campsite several miles out into the pasture.

Fort climbed out of his father's Blazer, his boots

grinding into the gravel of the driveway. He stretched his arms and legs, enjoying the warmth of the spring sunshine. The air carried a pungent mixture of barnyard smells, prairie hay and livestock manure. A windmill squeaked in the breeze. Chickens clucked from a wire pen. A cow bellowed in the distance.

A large black-and-brown dog trotted around the corner of the barn, then stopped and stared at Fort. He recognized the big-boned hound as a Rottweiler, then noticed the shiny spikes protruding from the dog's red-leather collar.

Not a good sign, thought Fort. He was tempted to climb back into the Blazer. Instead, he forced himself to stand firmly and hold his hand out toward the husky animal.

"Hello, boy," he said, as confidently as he could. "Come here, boy."

The dog inched forward and sniffed Fort's hand, then eagerly licked it. Fort patted the Rottweiler's muscular neck and shoulder. A set of tags dangled from the collar. One silvery tag was for a rabies vaccination, and the other was simply inscribed "Butch."

The big dog circled Fort playfully, then bounded into the grassy yard. Butch returned shortly with an old tennis ball, dropped it in front of Fort, and looked up at him with bright eyes. Fort picked up the slobbery ball and pitched it across the lawn. Butch raced after the ball, then trotted back to drop it in front of Fort again.

"Good dog," said Fort, as he patted him.

The side door of the minivan slid open and out streamed three boys. Three boys from the Blazer quickly joined them.

"Here, doggie!" yelled Timmy.

"Fort, can I throw the ball?" asked Chip.

"Can I pet the dog, too?"

"Hold it, guys!" yelled Fort. "Let the dog get to know you first."

Before Fort could stop them, the squealing boys rushed to the fierce-looking Rottweiler and tumbled over him in a pile.

Fort held his breath, expecting the surprised dog to attack the boys. Instead, Butch scrambled to his feet, squirmed with obvious delight, and licked the faces of the giggling boys as they tried to stand up.

Fort smiled and sighed as the boys and the dog chased each other around the yard.

A horse and rider trotted around the corner of the barn. The horse was beige, almost peach colored, with a creamy-white mane and tail—a palomino. The young female rider wore blue jeans, a red shirt, and a white straw hat. Fort recognized her as Tana Newton, a freshman from school. They were both in the same computer class, but Fort couldn't recall ever talking to her. Tana's long, dark-brown hair bounced as she rode.

As she approached, Fort could feel his nerves begin to jangle. Tana turned toward the younger boys and the dog as they roughhoused on the lawn.

"I see you've discovered Butch's secret," she said.

"What's th-that?" Fort's forehead suddenly felt very warm. He hoped his face hadn't turned red.

"He's really just a big teddy bear," said Tana. "He was supposed to be a watchdog, but he's too friendly. We put that scary collar on him so he'll at least look tough when strangers drive up."

Fort could feel his heart racing. He remembered Tana's freckled face, but hadn't noticed the sparkle in her eyes before now. "I-I d-didn't know you lived out h-here," he said, wishing he would quit stammering.

"I don't. This is my uncle's ranch. He's at a cattlemen's convention in Dallas this week. I came out here to keep Aunt Sally company, and to ride my horse. Brandy and I are practicing for the barrel race at the rodeo in Independence next weekend."

Tana leaned forward and gave the horse a friendly pat on the neck. "Come on back and watch, if you want." She reined the horse toward the barn.

Fort followed her behind the barn, where he could see three yellow barrels arranged in a wide triangle. Tana pulled a black-plastic stopwatch from her pocket and held it out to Fort.

"Would you time us?" she asked.

As he took the watch from her, Tana's soft, warm hand brushed his. A tingle zipped through his body. He froze.

"Ready . . . go!" said Tana.

He barely had time to get his thumb on the stopwatch button before Tana tapped the heels of her boots into the palomino's ribs.

The horse charged toward one of the barrels, hooves kicking up a shower of dirt. As they approached the barrel, the horse and rider leaned into a tight turn. They hardly slowed as they looped cleanly around the obstacle.

Brandy's powerful legs stretched to hurtle them even faster toward another barrel.

To Fort, they seemed to be moving at reckless, breakneck speed. But Tana appeared to be relaxed, eagerly leaning forward, then sideways, as they wheeled tightly past the second barrel. The mare's cream-colored tail streamed gracefully behind them as they rounded the last barrel.

Fort almost forgot to punch the stop button as girl

and horse flashed by him. Tana trotted Brandy back to Fort.

"How'd we do?"

"L-looked g-great to m-me," Fort said.

Tana giggled. "I mean the time, silly," she said.

"Oh." He didn't know what to say, so he held the stopwatch up for her to see.

"Eh—not bad," she said, "but we'll have to do better to win any prizes." Then, with a mischievous smile, she asked, "Want to give it a try? You *can* ride, can't you?"

Fort hesitated. He had ridden horses at his grandfather's farm and at summer camp. He wasn't sure, however, that he was ready for Brandy careening around those barrels, and he didn't want to embarrass himself in front of Tana.

"Ah, sure," he answered. "But I think I'll take it a little slower. You know—to start with."

"That's probably a good idea." Tana grinned as she swung down off the palomino and handed the reins to Fort.

He gently patted Brandy's forehead and long nose, letting the mare get to know him as he savored the sweet-sour smell of horse sweat and hair. Fort slipped the reins back over her head and neck and then held them lightly in his left hand as he clutched the leather-covered saddle horn. He slipped his left boot into the stirrup and pulled himself up, swinging his right leg over the saddle. The leather of the saddle creaked as he settled himself. The stirrups were set for Tana's shorter legs, so Fort just let his feet hang free.

"Do you want me to lengthen the stirrups?" asked Tana.

"Ah, no thanks," said Fort. "I'm used to riding bareback."

"Well—okay," said Tana, with a doubtful expression on her face.

Fort hadn't been on a horse for over a year and had forgotten how high above the ground a rider was. He patted Brandy's muscular neck, as much to comfort himself as to soothe the animal. Then, holding the leather reins lightly in his left hand, Fort gently tapped his heels into her ribs. She stepped forward slowly. They circled a cement water trough and a metal windmill. Next, Fort trotted Brandy through a lazy figure eight in the small pasture behind the barn.

Once he felt ready, Fort urged Brandy into a canter toward the barrels. Pulling back on the reins, he slowed the mare and steered her into a comfortable turn around the first barrel. Fort encouraged Brandy to go faster as they rounded the last two barrels. Enjoying the ride and feeling more confident, he spurred her with his heels. They raced toward Tana. Fort reined Brandy to the side so they would miss Tana and the barn by a safe margin.

The Rottweiler rounded the corner of the barn in front of Brandy and Fort. Six screaming boys followed the dog. Brandy veered sharply to the right, tipping Fort to the left.

He squeezed his legs tightly against the saddle as he tried to keep from toppling off. Knees digging into the hard leather, he grabbed the saddle horn with his right hand. His head and body teetered forward as she raced onward. Facing her churning legs while the ground streaked by in a blur, he froze in fear, imagining himself falling headfirst under the pounding hooves.

He forced himself to reach up and grab a handful of Brandy's mane and dragged himself upward as she raced across the pasture. Upright in the saddle again, Fort pulled on the reins until Brandy slowed to a trot. He took a deep breath and tried to steady his shaking hands, then guided his mount back to the barn.

"Bravo!" Tana yelled, a bright smile on her face as she clapped her hands. "I thought for sure you were going to fall off. You did very well."

Fort's heart was still pounding, his breath short. He smiled at Tana's praise.

Then he saw the younger boys clustered around Tana, laughing and making fun of him. He could feel blood rushing to his head. His vision blurred as he swung down off the horse and rushed to the boys. Fort grabbed Timmy by the collar and threw his red-haired brother sideways to the ground. The other boys yelled, but all Fort heard was the hollow echo of voices. Tommy stepped forward, his face scolding, finger wagging.

Fort punched Tommy in the belly and shoved him to the ground. Straddling his brother with his knees, he raised his fist to hit the boy again. Fort was knocked forward as Timmy leaped onto his back, wrapping his skinny legs around Fort's body, his thin arms snaking around Fort's neck. Fort's ear seared with pain as Timmy bit him. He screamed as he pulled Timmy loose, then flung him away.

Fort watched the younger boys turn and run, then held his bleeding ear until the pain subsided. Blood smeared his fingers. After a moment, his breathing returned to normal. Then he remembered Tana Newton. Embarrassed, he turned to face her. She was gone.

Thoughts of his encounter with Tana the previous day evaporated as Fort's right foot slipped, nearly causing him to fall. Looking down, he saw that his boot was smeared with what looked like green mud. Behind him was a circular cow pie over a foot in diameter and two inches thick.

Unlike the dried chips he had seen earlier, this one glistened with moisture and partially digested grass. The center of the patty was marred by a smeared boot print where he had stepped, then slid. The air was filled with the smell of fresh manure. Fort pursed his lips and frowned as he scraped his boot against the grass until it was nearly clean.

"Hey!" called a young male voice in the distance.

Fort spotted the younger boys several hundred feet ahead of him in the pasture on a wide, flat-topped hill. Obviously excited, they were pointing toward the north and yelling for Fort to join them.

CHAPTER SIX

Fort hurried up the hill to the three younger Scouts and looked in the direction they were pointing. To the north from the hilltop, miles of nearly pristine prairie stretched from horizon to horizon. The rolling grassland was checkered with steep ridges and gently sloping hills similar to the one on which they stood. This was cattle country, crisscrossed with miles of barbed-wire fence.

Fort breathed in the fresh aroma of rain-washed prairie. Goose bumps prickled his arms as he absorbed the panoramic view before him. In his mind he could picture the vast buffalo herds that once covered the land. For a moment he imagined that he was an Indian brave watching a wagon train of pioneers crossing the prairie.

The Scouts' chatter brought Fort back to their situation. After checking his compass, he set a brisk pace to the southwest. The younger boys followed cheerfully, though Fort sensed they were getting tired. As he plodded onward, he couldn't help thinking of little Billy, crying and holding his broken arm.

Again, Fort's mind flooded with self-disgust. Head throbbing, he fought the urge to scream, to run away and hide forever. Instead, he picked up a fist-sized rock and hurled it with all of his strength. The stone sailed over scrub oaks and small cedar trees before falling out of sight. He tried to imagine where it now lay. Was it in the grass, or under a tree?

Fort pried another chunk of limestone from the mud and pitched it in the same direction as the first stone. He imagined the second stone falling right next to the first one. No way, he thought. Then he recalled his football coach teaching the team new plays, "What you can imagine, you can do." Fort cast another rock into the distance and visualized it landing next to the other two.

He stopped. Maybe he could use the same technique to control his temper.

As he hiked onward, he tried to think of instances when he had lost his temper. One by one he relived those moments, but this time instead of exploding in rage, he maintained his composure. No matter what the insult or injury, real or imaginary, he reacted calmly to the situation.

He tried to think of his favorite movies—ones in which the hero kept his cool and saved the day against incredible odds. Cowboys facing ruthless gunslingers.

Undercover agents protecting the world from terrorists. Spaceship commanders saving the universe from evil aliens.

Fort pretended that when his temper flared, his blood actually heated, then boiled over if he lost control of himself. From this point onward, if he felt his temper rising, he would focus on cooling his blood until he was back in control of himself. In the worst situations, he would mentally chill his blood even further and fill his veins with cold-blooded resolve.

Suddenly realizing he was well ahead of the younger boys, he stopped until they caught up. The gray clouds were starting to break apart, revealing patches of blue sky, and a gentle breeze caressed his cheeks. He took a deep breath of the fresh air, checked his compass, then continued his trek.

As Fort and the Scouts hiked toward the south and west, the terrain became rougher and sported more outcroppings of rock. Patches of prairie began to be surrounded by mature cedars and Blackjack oaks. Fort rounded a tree and nearly bumped into Booger, Jonathan, and Tommy, who were backing toward him. The boys turned, their eyes wide with fear. Over their heads, Fort saw the reason for their alarm.

Less than twenty feet in front of them stood a full-grown Hereford bull. It stared straight at Fort, muscles bulging through its reddish-brown coat. Foot-long horns curved out from each side of the animal's huge white-haired head. It snorted, lowered its head menacingly, and stepped closer.

Fort's heart pounded as adrenalin coursed through him. "Stay perfectly still," he instructed the boys as quietly as he could. If the bull charged them, they would be in serious trouble. There were no fences in sight and no trees big enough to climb. The bull could outrun them. Its rock-hard head could ram them, its thick, pointed horns could gore them, and its sharp hooves could stomp them. If it attacked, one or more of the Scouts could either be killed or lie maimed and bleeding before the bull finished with them.

The bull sniffed the air as it eyed the Scouts. It snorted again and lowered its head. It grabbed a clump of grass with its mouth, and yanked its head sideways to tear off a big bite. It raised its head again, calmly chewing the grass and staring directly at the boys. Then the bull dipped its head once more, took a small step to the side, and continued grazing. It ignored the young humans.

Beyond the bull, Fort could see dozens of grazing cows, also Herefords. Some of them chewed lazily as they, too, eyed the boys. Tiny, reddish-brown calves with curly white heads frolicked among the adults. One calf suckled milk from its mother as she grazed.

Fort reached forward and tapped Booger's shoulder, then backed a cautious step away from the bull. The animal raised its head to watch, but continued feeding. Beckoning the boys to follow, Fort kept a wary eye on the bull as they eased back around the tree.

Once they were again in the brush, Fort paused to check on the Scouts. Their faces were pale. He laughed, more from nervous relief than humor. "Let's get out of here. Fast!" He started to run.

Picking a course with relatively little brush, he sprinted ahead. He hurdled a clump of weeds and jumped over a small bush. Trees, brush, and weeds flowed by in a blur. He could hear the boys following him.

Running cleared Fort's mind. His problems seemed to fall behind him as he raced up a gentle slope to a rocky ledge. Breathing hard, he scrambled to the highest outcropping.

Once again, to the north the endless panorama of prairie spread before him. Relieved of fear and revitalized by fresh air and exercise, he raised his arms, looked to the far northern horizon, and yelled. The sound soared out across the prairie.

Between gray clouds, he could see a patch of blue with the straight white line of a jet's contrail etched across it. Probably a jetliner heading from one coast to the other, he thought, then wondered if anyone happened to be looking down at him from one of the clear-acrylic airliner windows. For a moment, Fort wished he were miles above the earth and heading to a distant destination.

Boot soles grating on rock and heavy breathing signaled the arrival of the younger boys. Fort resented their intrusion. Then he remembered his father and Billy. And he wondered how his mom was doing. He took one more look at the vast prairie scene and the distant vapor trail, then sighed and checked his compass.

Turning toward the southwest, he warily searched the tree-cluttered pasture for more cattle. Seeing none, he set off in a direction that he hoped would soon lead them to the ranch house. The Scouts chattered and teased each other as they walked.

"Fort," asked Booger, his index finger twisting around in his ear, "why didn't that bull charge us? I always thought bulls were mean."

"They can be," said Fort, as he watched Booger extract a pea-sized lump of orange wax from one ear, then flip it out into the brush. "And since they're so big and powerful, they can do a lot of damage. But they're not always mean. Only when they get angry or feel threatened."

"Threatened?" asked freckle-faced Jonathan, with a laugh. "That thing was huge. What could possibly threaten it?"

"Well, nothing out here, really," said Fort. "But sometimes they just go berserk over nothing."

Tommy laughed. "Fort, that sounds like you!"

Fort stopped. His face turned hot, and the arteries in his neck throbbed.

Tommy's smile melted. He turned and fled, and the other boys raced after him. After they disappeared into the trees, Fort heard their nervous giggling.

Ashamed, he reminded himself that gaining control over his temper might be a long-term challenge. The suggestion that he was like a dangerous bull had angered and embarrassed him, but maybe the idea wasn't so far-fetched. He hurried to catch up to the other boys.

They continued their trek through increasingly dense trees and brush. At first, Fort saw little sign of the late-night storm. As they continued farther south and west, however, he noticed more trash and debris—scraps of paper and tin cans, mutilated boards, and corrugated metal.

The small trees began to look more and more mangled. They walked past a flattened metal grain storage bin, a soaked mattress, and a ripped-and-muddy sofa chair. Spiky strands of barbed wire, with wood fence posts still attached, dangled from twisted tree limbs. They passed uprooted trees. A circular saw blade had somehow become embedded in a stout fence post. Fort kept his growing concern to himself.

Tommy looked up at Fort. "Does Grandpa have bulls on his farm?"

"Sometimes the male calves are still bulls when he buys them," said Fort, "but they get castrated."

"Castrated?" asked Booger. "What's that?"

"You idiot," said Jonathan. "You don't know what 'castrated' means?"

"Easy, guys," said Fort. "If you've lived in town all your life, like we have, you may not know these things. Booger—I mean, Roger, 'castrate' means that the animal's testicles are removed. Sometimes my grandma saves them so we can have mountain oysters for dinner."

"Mountain what?" asked Booger.

"Mountain oysters. When you cut out the testicles, you can deep fry 'em in oil like French fries." Fort smiled and rubbed his belly. "Yum, yum." He laughed at the horrified looks on the other boys' faces.

"That's gross," said Jonathan. "I think I'm gonna puke."

"That sounds so mean," Booger said. "Why do they have to castrate them, anyway?"

"Bulls," answered Fort, "get male hormones from their testicles that make them big, powerful, and aggressive. Steers—that's what they're called after they're castrated —become more relaxed. They gain weight faster. They get fat, and that's what makes beef tender. Bull meat can be tough."

The storm debris became so thick that they had to slow their pace to maneuver around the larger items. Fort hoped they were getting close to the ranch house. A pair of large, mangled cedar trees blocked his way.

He stepped around them into a wide clearing, but stopped short when he heard a squawk. The air in front of him suddenly filled with beating black wings. Fort stumbled backwards, arms raised to protect his face, as a huge black bird flapped its powerful wings to gain height quickly. The head of the surprised bird was featherless and covered with gnarled red skin. Fort recognized it as a turkey vulture.

Fort took a breath to calm himself, then wondered what had so preoccupied the buzzard. Cautiously, he pulled the cedar branches aside and peeked around them. Beyond the fallen tree lay the carcass of a black horse.

The younger boys elbowed past Fort and quickly circled the bloated, stiff-legged horse. Two legs didn't even touch the ground, as if the horse had suddenly frozen solid, then tipped over on its side. Dried blood trailed from its mouth and nose. Fort couldn't see any obvious wounds or even vulture bites. He assumed the buzzard would begin with the eyes and mouth, or the soft tissue of the other orifices. Just thinking about the buzzard gave him the creeps.

Flies swarmed in an angry buzz, and Fort noticed the ripe smell already filling the air around the black horse. The stench left a putrid taste in his mouth. He gathered his saliva, then turned to the side and spat.

Booger stepped toward the horse with a stick and tapped the mud-smeared hair on the dead animal's side. "What happened to it?"

"Well, duh! What do you think?" asked Jonathan. "There was a tornado last night."

Booger waved the stick in front of the horse's bloody nose, and black flies buzzed away briefly before returning to the oozing body fluids. The boy poked the stick into the horse's open nostril, then stepped back and looked at the blood.

"What are you looking for now?" asked Tommy.

"Maggots," said Booger. "I thought dead animals

were filled with maggots."

"It's too soon," said Jonathan. "The flies aren't just eating the blood, they're laying eggs. The eggs will hatch into little white worms. The worms are larva, or maggots. They eat the rotting meat, and eventually grow into flies—the way caterpillars grow into butterflies."

"Do you mean this whole horse is going to be eaten by maggots?" Tommy looked appalled.

Fort tried to imagine the entire horse becoming a maggot-infested carcass of rotting meat. "More likely the maggots will eat some of it, and the coyotes, possums, and vultures will eat the rest," he said. "Unless somebody hauls it away, within a few months there won't be anything left of this horse except a few scattered bones." He grinned. "So you'd better hurry if you're hungry for some horse meat."

Booger grimaced and threw the stick to the ground.

"Fort," stammered Tommy, "sometimes I think you're sick."

Fort looked back at the dead horse before leaving. At least it isn't Brandy, he thought. Then he remembered Mr. Crawford's body wrapped in a blue tarp and the three eleven-year-olds and his father he had left with the corpse. Better hurry.

As he scanned the territory ahead, his heart nearly stopped. The open space before them wasn't just another clearing in the brush, he realized. The scattered trash in front of him was all that remained of the Newton ranch house and barn.

CHAPTER SEVEN

Fort swallowed hard and blinked. He stepped toward the demolished ranch buildings and carefully picked his way around hundreds of shattered wooden boards, many with pointed, rusty nails exposed.

"Tana!" he called. "Mrs. Newton!"

He smiled as Butch emerged from behind a fallen tree and trotted toward them. Fort patted his own thigh and called the dog's name, expecting Butch to greet him. Instead, the Rottweiler barked and growled.

Trying again, Fort cheerfully called the dog's name, then held out his hand in friendship. The dog barked louder and snarled. He had heard of animals driven crazy by storms that destroyed their homes and disoriented them. Sometimes the animals became violent.

"Stay back," he told the boys.

The Rottweiler barked again and edged closer. Booger suddenly turned and ran. The black-and-brown dog darted forward, quickly catching the boy's leg. Booger tumbled to the ground, the big dog on top of him. The Rottweiler shook his head from side to side as his jaws crunched into the boy's leg. Booger screamed, his arms and legs thrashing.

The dog released the boy's leg and lunged for Booger's exposed throat as if he was trying to rip out the boy's windpipe and jugular vein, going for a kill. Fort leaped, headfirst and arms extended, toward the Rottweiler.

His flying tackle knocked the dog off Booger. Fort and the dog tumbled over each other on the muddy ground. The Rottweiler scrambled to his feet, ears back against his head. Then he snarled, showing sharp, yellow teeth.

Fort struggled to his feet. As the dog charged, Fort raised his forearm in defense. Dagger-sharp teeth ripped into the muscle of his arm as the impact of the charging dog sent him sprawling backward into the mud.

Fort sprang upright, scooped his hands under the dog, and heaved him up and away. The Rottweiler cartwheeled in the air before flopping into the mud with a yelp of pain.

Butch scrambled to his feet, then charged again. Fort stooped and grabbed a loose piece of wood—a two-by-four. He swung hard as the Rottweiler leaped toward him. The board hit the dog's head with a thud, and then the hound's forward momentum knocked

Fort on his back.

The Rottweiler scrambled to his feet and lunged for Fort's throat. Fort caught the dog's snout with both hands and squeezed, clamping its mouth shut. Butch's claws raked Fort's legs and belly. Fort wrapped his own legs around the Rottweiler's churning hindquarters.

Still holding the dog's mouth tightly with one hand, Fort slipped his other arm around the Rottweiler's back and squeezed, pressing the dog's chest against his own. Now he held the crazed dog pinned on the muddy ground, his right arm wrapped around the chest and forelegs of the animal. Ankles locked, Fort's legs were scissored tightly around the dog's belly and hips.

Butch showed no sign of tiring. Fort, however, could feel his own muscles growing numb as he fought to maintain his hold on the growling, squirming dog. He could hear Booger crying somewhere nearby. His mind raced. If the dog wiggled free, or if Fort let it go, it would attack him or the younger boys again. He feared, though, that his own muscles would give out long before the powerful Rottweiler weakened.

Fort could feel blood rush to his head and his vision blur. In a flash, he could see the moments ahead. He would force the dog's head back, exposing its throat. Then he would bite through the Rottweiler's neck, going for the kill himself. His teeth would rip through the dog's jugular vein, then crush and tear through the windpipe. Foamy red blood would spray Fort's face as life gushed out of the mad dog.

Fort shuddered to think he might be capable of such savagery. He tried to slow his breathing and to cool the blood he imagined to be boiling within him. His mind cleared, and he realized he was in control again. He crushed the Rottweiler to himself as the dog snarled and squirmed. Fort knew he could—and would—kill the dog to protect himself and the younger boys, if necessary. He was running out of strength and had only one other option to try.

"Butch," Fort whispered. "Calm down, boy."

The dog growled under Fort's grip and strained to get free.

"It's okay, Butch," said Fort. "You're a good dog."

Fort continued to speak softly to the dog, but time seemed endless before he could feel the animal relax. Its struggles and growls slowed, then stopped.

After releasing one hand cautiously, Fort gently stroked the Rottweiler's head. The dog whined. Fort was thoroughly exhausted. His arms and legs couldn't hold on any longer. He relaxed the hand clamped over the dog's snout. The Rottweiler squirmed free and was on top of Fort almost instantly—its snout and teeth at Fort's face.

Butch's thick, slimy tongue darted across Fort's nose. Fort lay helplessly on his back as the dog licked his face. After a moment Fort sat up and pushed the big animal to the side, then wiped slobber from his face with his bleeding forearm. He spit on the ground. "Yuck!"

Fort could see the younger boys watching at a distance. Before he could stop the dog, Butch rushed toward the eleven-year-olds. Fort saw them panic, then scramble to escape the Rottweiler. Booger was still on the ground and struggling to get up when Butch reached him. The dog knocked Booger onto his back, then held him down with a paw as he eagerly licked the boy's face.

Fort's daypack was just a few feet away, and he dragged himself to it. After calling Booger closer, he rinsed the boy's bites with water from a bottle and cleaned them as best as he could. He squeezed some antiseptic ointment out of a small tube and carefully spread it over the open wounds before applying Band-Aids.

Pain brought Fort's attention back to himself. An angry, red gash on his forearm throbbed and bled. The small first-aid kit contained only a few bandages, none of them big enough to cover the entire bite. He wrapped his red tee shirt over his forearm and tucked the ends under to hold it in place.

"Fort, I hear somebody!" Tommy pointed to what remained of the ranch house.

Fort quickly surveyed the farm site. An old, white Ford pickup lay upside down, its windows shattered. The ranch house and barn were a trail of splintered timber and household items haphazardly strewn toward the north and east. Only the cement foundations remained in their original location. The chicken house and metal grain bins were gone, but chickens pecked and clucked around the farmyard.

Fort stood still and listened. He heard the voice, too—a faint cry for help.

"It's from the basement!" cried Jonathan.

Fort started toward the remains of the house.

"Hold it!" yelled Tommy. "We need to be careful. There may be electrical wires on the ground. We won't be much help to anyone if we get ourselves electrocuted."

Fort stopped. Tommy was right, of course, but it annoyed him that his little brother had thought of it first. His forehead throbbed. He took a deep breath and exhaled slowly. After a moment, he turned to Tommy and said, "Good thinking."

Tommy beamed.

Fort studied the rubble around them. Wires seemed to be everywhere—barbed wire and woven wire for livestock fence, baling wire for hay, and electrical wire.

"We can turn the electricity off," said Fort, "if we can find the circuit-breaker box. It might have been in the house, or there could be an electric utility pole outside somewhere."

"Oh, sure, Fort," said Jonathan. "How are we going to find a breaker box in this pile of junk? Besides, at our house the breaker box is in the basement."

"Never mind, guys." Fort pointed down the driveway where a broken utility pole leaned halfway to the ground, a short stub of electrical line dangling from a brown-ceramic insulator. "The wire is broken out there," he said, "so there's no electricity here right now, but unless you want to get electrocuted, stay away from those poles, okay?"

The boys nodded.

"Hey, Fort," asked Booger, "what are the wires on the shorter poles?"

Fort studied the other utility poles a moment before answering. "Unfortunately, those are the telephone lines."

"If the telephone lines are broken," asked Tommy,

"how are we going to call for help?"

Fort felt like screaming. He took a deep breath, then answered with a sigh. "I guess we won't be able to call home from here, will we? We'll just have to figure out something else."

"What's that smell?" Booger asked.

Jonathan wrinkled his nose. "All I smell is the barnyard."

Fort sniffed the air and listened. "That's propane," he said. "I don't hear a hissing sound, but I definitely smell gas. If we're not careful we could cause an explosion. Even a small spark might set it off. Do you see a gas meter anywhere?"

Not hearing an answer, Fort turned to see the younger boys were already dragging tree limbs off a large, white metal tank at the edge of a ruined garden. Fort hustled over and gently tipped open a helmet-shaped cap on the top.

"What is this thing?" asked Jonathan. "It looks like a baby submarine."

Fort laughed and then studied the pipes and valves extending from the top of the propane tank. He identified the shut-off valve and turned it off.

The boys were exploring the house foundation, calling for Mrs. Newton and Tana. A faint reply emerged from the open basement. Fort saw that the basement floor was buried beneath a mixture of shattered timber and red chimney bricks. There was no sign of either Tana or her aunt.

"They're in there somewhere, guys," he said as he edged around the foundation. "Everybody look carefully."

A picture of Tana lying crushed and bleeding under a pile of rubble flashed through his mind. He couldn't bear the thought of Tana in pain, suffering, or dead. He called for her again, but heard nothing.

They had almost circled the foundation when Booger yelled and pointed at an old-fashioned set of basement steps that had apparently collapsed under the weight of the fallen chimney. Moving closer, Fort saw an arm extending from under the stairs—a mature woman's arm, not Tana's.

He started to climb down into the basement, but stopped when he saw the needle-sharp tips of splintered wood piled below him. Bare patches of concrete were exposed here and there around the basement, so he edged over to the one closest to the fallen stairs. He scooted across the gritty foundation and then dropped to the basement floor.

The smell of propane filled the air. Fort realized that the women might have been lucky that the floor of the house was gone so the gas hadn't accumulated to a dangerous level. He hoped it would disperse quickly now that the line was turned off at the tank. The breeze outside would also help, he reasoned.

Between him and the collapsed stairs was a waist-high pile of broken timber spiked with nails. Fort looked up to the boys peering down at him from the top of the foundation. "You'd better stay there till I clear this out."

He picked up a board and tossed it out of the way. Then, remembering that he still didn't know where Tana was, he selected another bare spot in the floor as his target and began pitching wood and bricks as fast as he could pick them up.

Soon he had worked his way through the debris to the staircase. He reached out and touched the woman's wrist. It was warm. He felt for a pulse. She was still alive—unconscious, but breathing. As Fort carefully cleared broken boards and bricks away from the woman, he called, "Tana!"

A weak voice replied, "Help me . . . please."

Relief washed through Fort, but was quickly replaced with panic. Tana must be under the stairs, too, he realized. He began to pull bricks and loose boards off the steps.

"Hold on, Tana," he called. "I'll get you out."

Fort tried to lift the collapsed stairs. They wouldn't

budge. The three younger Scouts had been watching him quietly from above. Now they scrambled into the cellar. Together, the four pulled up on the staircase. It lifted only an inch or two. As they lowered it back down, Tana screamed.

Fort let loose a stream of profanity. Eyes wild, he picked up a brick and hurled it across the cellar. The basement echoed as the brick hit some timber, then thumped to the floor. He bent over, hands on his knees, until his breathing slowed and his mind cleared.

"Tana," he said. "I'll be right back." Turning to the Scouts, he said, "You guys stay here. See if you can wake Mrs. Newton, but don't try to move her."

"Where are you going?" asked Booger, his voice shaky, his lower lip quivering.

Fort ruffled the younger boy's hair. "Don't worry, I'll be right back." He climbed out of the basement.

After a few minutes he returned with a long, thick wooden beam that had formed part of the barn's frame. He maneuvered the four-inch-square piece of timber down to the boys and then dropped back into the basement.

"This will be our lever. Now we need a fulcrum." He spotted a hefty section of bricks still cemented together in a block and shoved it closer to the stairs. He lifted the heavy beam and laid it across the section of bricks, then carefully poked one end under the stairs. He shoved another block of bricks close to the steps.

"Tommy," said Fort, "as soon as we lever the stairs high enough, you be ready to push this section of bricks underneath to hold them up."

Under Fort's direction, Jonathan and Booger sat on the end of the long lever while Fort pushed downward. The stairs moved only a little.

"Hold it." Fort relaxed his grip on the long beam. "We're going to need more weight on this end."

He picked up another big block of bricks and balanced it on the raised end of the beam until Jonathon scooted forward to hold it in place with his legs.

Fort crawled up behind the boys. He could feel the timber bend under the increased weight, and he made a silent prayer that the old beam wouldn't break.

"It's moving!" cried Tommy.

Slowly, the staircase rose as the lever seesawed downward on Fort's end. The four-by-four creaked and groaned.

Fort held his breath.

Tommy grunted as he pushed on his block of bricks. Fort could hear it grinding against the gritty floor.

"Okay, Fort," yelled Tommy. "They're under the stairs."

Fort was ready to step down when the beam snapped. He tumbled to the floor with Booger and Jonathan. Then he scrambled back up to check on Tana and Mrs. Newton. The stairs were now propped a foot higher than earlier. Mrs. Newton still lay on the floor, but the stairs were no longer crushing down on her body.

Tana crawled out from under the wooden staircase. Dust and grit powdered her face and clothes. Cobwebs dangled from her hair. Fort saw no obvious injuries, but noticed a vacant look in her eyes.

Tana's expression changed instantly when she looked toward Mrs. Newton. "Aunt Sally!" she said, as she crawled over to her. "Are you okay?"

The woman's eyelids flickered. Her mouth opened as if she was about to speak.

Fort crawled closer.

The woman's eyes closed, and she winced. "Oooo-oh," she moaned. "It hurts."

Tana clasped her aunt's hand and raised it to her own cheek.

After a moment, Fort took a deep breath. "Mrs. Newton, I'm Fort Curtis—one of the Boy Scouts who camped out in your pasture last night. Remember, you talked to my dad and Mr. Crawford yesterday?"

The woman's eyes opened. She stared at Fort. "You're the one with the bad temper," she said.

Fort felt as if he had been slapped in the face. "Y-yes," he said, "I do have a temper."

Tana turned and looked questioningly up at Fort.

He looked directly into her eyes. "But I'm learning to control it." He spoke to Mrs. Newton. "Right now, let's worry about you. It's very important that you lie still. Can you tell me where it hurts?"

The woman licked her lips, then swallowed. Suddenly, her eyes opened wide. "I can't feel my legs!" she wailed, thrashing from side to side. "Get me out of here!" She pressed her arms against the floor and tried to rise, then dropped back on the cement floor with a groan.

"Mrs. Newton," said Fort, as confidently as he could, "you're going to be fine." He put his hand on the woman's shoulder. "Just lie still and rest. We're going to get help here as soon as possible."

Mrs. Newton's face relaxed and her eyes closed. Her mouth opened slightly as her head turned to the side.

"Aunt Sally?" said Tana. She leaned forward and yelled again. "Aunt Sally!"

Fort eased Tana aside, then leaned over Mrs.

Newton and placed his ear close to her mouth. He could feel and hear shallow-but-steady breathing.

"She just fainted," he said. "Talk to her. Pat her on the cheek, gently. She should wake up in a little while." Fort hoped that he was right. He paused, trying to remember the first aid for a back injury. "Tana," he said, "it's very important that your aunt lie still when she wakes up. Can you keep her calm and quiet?"

Tana clutched her aunt's hand tightly and nodded.

Fort heard a noise behind him, and he spun around to see the three younger Scouts standing quietly, eyes wide. He had nearly forgotten them.

"Guys, we have lots to do. I'm going to need your help. Let's climb back out of here."

CHAPTER EIGHT

Fort grabbed an armload of damp prairie hay and tossed it on top of the bonfire. A plume of white smoke surged toward the gray sky. He had centered the fire on the wide gravel parking lot of the farmstead, far from the basement and anything that might accidentally catch fire. The younger boys eagerly tossed sticks and lumber onto the flames.

Looking up, Fort realized the low, gray clouds would make it difficult for anyone to see the white smoke. He suspected that the police, fire, and ambulance personnel in the area were overwhelmed by the devastation in the city of Strickler. The Scouts might have little chance of getting help anytime soon.

Fort searched the debris-covered barnyard until he found an old tire. He lugged it to the parking lot and heaved it onto the signal fire. A wisp of black smoke snaked upward, and he caught a whiff of burning rubber. The thread of black quickly grew into a column. A gentle breeze tilted the expanding plume toward the northeast.

"Awesome," said Jonathan.

"It looks like a tornado," said Booger.

Fort gazed skyward. Booger's right, he thought. The massive black plume surging toward the clouds looked much like the funnel-shaped images he had seen on TV.

"Guys," said Fort, "this black smoke should be visible for many miles. If we're going to get any help, we need to get somebody's attention."

"Won't that pollute the air?" asked Tommy,

Fort felt a surge of blood rush to his head. He took a step toward Tommy—then stopped. He exhaled a long, slow breath.

"Sometimes desperate situations call for desperate measures," he answered evenly, hoping he was doing the right thing.

He had already rechecked the bandages on Booger's bite wounds and tied Butch to a tree stump. The Rottweiler seemed to be himself again, but Fort wanted to be sure the dog didn't hurt anyone else. Booger had found a small piece of broken mirror and was ready to use it as a signal if they saw an airplane.

Fort sipped from his canteen, worried that they would run out of water before help arrived. With the windmill and the electricity gone, there was no source of clean water at the ranch house. He pulled a metal bucket from a pile of debris, rinsed it in the stock tank, then scooped out a bucketful of murky, green water. Tiny insects swam frantically amid floating algae as the water sloshed around in the bucket.

He set the pail at the edge of the fire, wishing he had a water-purification filter or tablets. Boiling the water should kill the germs and other floating wildlife, he hoped, and they could pour the boiled water through a cloth to filter out the bugs and debris. Still, the water would probably be gritty, with a greenish tint and fishy taste—and he wasn't certain it would be safe to drink.

The inside of his mouth suddenly puckered and felt dry. "Hey, guys," he yelled. "Let's conserve the water in our canteens to make it last as long as we can."

He climbed back down into the basement and sat, legs crossed, on the cool, concrete floor near Mrs. Newton and Tana.

"Mrs. Newton," he said, gently pressing her shoulder, "I know the highway is several miles south of the creek. Is there any way I can get across the creek when it's flooded?"

The woman's eyes were barely open. She shook her head slowly. "Too dangerous," she said weakly, then closed her eyes.

Fort looked at Tana.

"She keeps passing out," said Tana. "The pain

must be terrible."

"I'm going down to the creek to take a look," said Fort. "The boys can watch your aunt for a while, if you want to come along."

Before Tana could answer, Jonathan peered over the top of the basement foundation.

"We're hungry," he said. "Is there any food down there?"

Fort turned to Tana. "Does your aunt keep an emergency food supply?"

Tana glanced around the rubble-filled basement and shook her head. "As far as I know, all the food was upstairs in the kitchen."

Fort hadn't seen any food that looked edible in the wreckage outside. Butch had gobbled up the few scraps that had been scattered across the barnyard. Fort had noticed an empty feeling in his stomach, too, but he hadn't taken the time to do anything about it. He knew that they could survive for weeks without food. He also knew they would all get cranky and tired if they didn't eat soon. And who knew how long they would be stuck out here?

Fort looked up at Jonathan. "Have you ever caught a chicken?"

The boy surveyed the barnyard. Then his face lit up with excitement. "Fort says we can catch some chickens!" he yelled.

Fort could hear running footsteps and boys screaming and laughing, soon followed by an excited cackle of chickens. He smiled, remembering the first time he had chased chickens on his grandparents' farm. He had been amazed at the speed and agility of the birds. He turned back to Tana and Mrs. Newton. "I'll be back in a little while."

He stepped off the house foundation as the younger boys were running up to him. Each boy clutched a struggling chicken to his chest. The birds squawked and clawed as the boys tried to control them.

Fort laughed. "Here, let me show you how to hold them." He grabbed the legs of Jonathan's chicken. "Now, let go."

The bird struggled, legs jerking and wings flapping, as Fort held it upside down by its legs. Soon the chicken grew tired and hung quietly in Fort's grip.

Tommy grabbed his chicken by the legs and held it until it calmed.

Booger's bird flapped and clawed as the boy tried to reach its legs. Suddenly the chicken was free, beating its wings as it dropped to the ground and raced away. Booger yelled and ran after it.

"Hold it!" called Fort. "Two chickens should be

plenty."

He looked around the cluttered farmyard. The chances of finding a hatchet were pretty slim. Then he remembered how his grandmother had butchered chickens on the farm.

Fort picked up a two-foot length of lumber and walked over to a board lying on the ground. Holding the struggling bird out in front of him, its neck over the board, Fort laid the smaller board across the top of the chicken's neck. He quickly stepped on one end of the board, then placed his other foot on the other end of the board.

He tightened his grip on the bird's legs and pulled, quickly and powerfully, severing the chicken's head from its neck. Blood squirted and sprayed as Fort heaved the carcass away from him.

He held his hand out to Tommy, who was holding the remaining chicken, but the boy was staring at the bloody head lying in the grass. Fort picked up the chicken's severed head—its eyes blinking, its beak opening and closing—and tossed it to Butch.

The dog stepped forward cautiously, sniffed, then gulped the head in one motion. Butch's big tongue slurped from one side of his mouth to the other as he sat on his haunches looking to Fort, eyes bright with anticipation of another treat.

Again, Fort held his hand out to Tommy. The boy recoiled, clutching his chicken closer and stepping back.

"I'm sorry, Tommy," said Fort. "This grosses me out, too. It's better not to think about it—just get it over with. We need food, and these chickens are all we have."

Fort held his hand out toward the boy again. Tommy glanced at the bird in his arms, then looked sorrowfully up at Fort and handed over the chicken.

Fort turned, quickly decapitated the bird, and tossed it out onto the grass with the other one. Both birds flapped their wings and leaped into the air, over and over again—headless bodies fleeing danger. Fort remembered watching a dozen chickens flopping at one time as he helped his grandmother butcher them. He had been amazed at how long their legs jumped and wings beat before they finally lay motionless.

He shuddered and walked to the stock tank, where he scooped up slimy water with both hands and sloshed it over his face. He felt tired, thirsty, and hungry, and they were running out of time. He had to get back to Timmy, Chip, and Billy, and find help for his dad and Mrs. Newton.

Fort walked back to the fire and returned with the bucket of boiling water. "Okay, guys," he asked, "who wants to pluck the chickens?"

The look on the younger boys' faces told Fort they wouldn't be any help, so he picked up one of the dead chickens and grabbed a handful of feathers. He pulled hard, but only a couple of small feathers came loose. "Now watch," he said.

He picked up both birds by their legs and dunked them into the steaming water, then swished them around in the bucket for a few moments. The air filled with the pungent aroma of scalded feathers.

Fort lifted one of the birds out of the water and grabbed a handful of steaming feathers. This time they pulled easily from the carcass. He let the feathers fall to the ground, ignoring the blistering heat as he grabbed another handful. All three of the younger boys quickly huddled around Fort.

"Let me," said Jonathan, holding his hand toward the dead chicken. Each of the boys took turns until the ground was littered with feathers and both birds were stripped to naked carcasses.

Fort pulled out his pocketknife and cut the chickens' legs off at the knees, then tossed the legs to Butch. He sliced open a bird's rear end, pulled the flesh apart, and shoved his hand into the chicken's warm, slippery body cavity. He grabbed a big handful of squishy intestines and pulled them out of the carcass.

As Fort tossed the steaming guts to Butch, the air was filled with a smell that reminded Fort of both manure and vomit. Images of his grandmother flashed through his mind. She would probably laugh if she knew that the smells of butchering reminded him of her. He would always miss her.

The Scouts were watching Fort closely. "Want to try this?" he asked. The boys backed away, shaking their heads and making disgusted faces.

Fort reached inside the bird again and pulled out another handful of entrails. He studied the slippery, sticky mass in his hand for a second before slicing out a reddish-brown organ. He held the piece up to the boys. "Do any of you like chicken livers? They're delicious."

Booger's eyes rolled. His knees buckled, and he collapsed onto the grass.

Fort looked to the other boys. "He'll be okay." He kept an eye on the unconscious boy as he finished gutting the birds.

Booger regained consciousness shortly and sat, legs folded, on the grass.

"Okay, guys," said Fort. "One more question for you. Do you want your chicken baked or roasted?"

"I like mine Kentucky Fried," said Jonathan.

"Sorry." Fort smiled. "We don't have a fry cooker. How about if we bake one and roast the other?"

He hurried over to a storm-damaged tree and broke off a branch about a half-inch thick. He sharpened one end of the stick, forced it through a bird's carcass, and handed the skewered bird to Tommy.

Fort searched the storm debris before selecting two rusty wheel rims. Laying each of the heavy metal rims at the edge of the fire, he balanced the skewered chicken between them. "That will be our roast chicken," he said. "Now let's bake one."

He carried the second chicken to the vegetable garden behind the propane tank and placed it on the muddy ground. Thrusting his fingers and hands into the rich brown soil, he gathered a huge ball of mud. He patted and punched the big ball until it was bowl shaped, laid the lifeless chicken inside, and carefully closed the sides of the bowl around the bird until it was encased in mud.

Fort brought his homemade roaster back to the fire. Shielding his face from the heat, he positioned the big mud ball on the hot coals near the fire's edge. He jumped back and rubbed the scorched hair on the back his hands. Burned hair joined the growing mixture of smells around him.

"It'll probably take an hour or more to cook," he said, "but we'll have chicken for lunch."

"I think I'll just wait till we're rescued," said Jonathan.

Fort laughed. "Suit yourself—but you said you were hungry."

CHAPTER
NINE

Tana clutched Fort's arm as she hobbled beside him along the gravel lane that connected the ranch to the rest of the world. They reached the rocky crest of a small hill overlooking the tree-lined creek. Fort steadied Tana as she took a seat on an outcropping of weathered limestone.

The day before, the road had sloped down to the rocky creek bed and a wide slab of concrete that served as a bridge across the trickle of water that flowed most of the year. Today, a river of floodwater rolled through the little valley.

Fort watched the driftwood and debris bobbing erratically in the wide circle of a gentle eddy near the shore. Farther out, half-submerged cottonwoods quivered, leaves quaking green and silver, as tons of water surged by. At mid-channel where the current ran fastest, driftwood sped downstream.

Looking more closely, Fort could see whirlpools of brown water spinning around tree trunks and at the edge of the fast-moving flow. Liquid cyclones would whirl for a moment and then quickly disappear as the current whisked them away, only to be replaced by others. Fort knew that conflicting currents could also create undertows capable of dragging a person down to a watery death.

He listened to the hiss of the floodwaters, a whisper with a deep-but-subtle rumble underneath. For a moment his stomach ached as he imagined the flood was alive—a menacing, evil being eager to destroy him. He shook that thought off, but still watched the current warily.

He felt Tana tug at the tee shirt covering the dog bite on his forearm and realized the makeshift bandage had come undone. His skin tingled at her touch, and he felt his breath grow short as she unwound the red shirt and retied it.

For a few moments Fort and Tana just watched the swollen creek as it flowed by. Then Fort's thoughts returned to their situation. The concrete bridge must be many feet under the floodwaters. "Is there another bridge?" he asked.

Tana shook her head. "Years ago, there was a big bridge farther downstream," she said, "but it was washed out. The county government decided not to fix it—too expensive, they said." She sighed. "Now, when it floods like this, my aunt and uncle just stay home until the water recedes. Then they can drive across the low-water bridge."

"Any idea how long it will be before the bridge is passable again?" asked Fort.

Tana shrugged. "I was out here last spring when we were flooded in for a couple of days."

"What about to the west," asked Fort, "across the Elk River? Does any bridge cross there?"

Tana cocked her head for a moment before answering. "Only far from us."

Fort already knew the creek was impassable for miles upstream, where they had been camping.

"So," he said, thinking out loud, "this creek is flooded all the way to the Elk River. The river is even deeper and wider than this creek, and there aren't any bridges we can use." He faced Tana. "How about to the north? Is there some place we can go for help? Neighbors? A telephone?"

Tana looked Fort in the eyes. "You were just out there, Fort," she answered. "This is one of the most isolated parts of the whole state. Some people are even trying to turn it into a national park to preserve the prairie." She shook her head. "I'm sorry, but there isn't much out there but grass and cattle for nearly twenty miles." She turned toward the pasture. "Did you see Brandy? She must've been spooked by the storm and run away."

Fort told Tana about the dead horse, and then wished he hadn't. "I'm sure Brandy is just fine," he said quickly.

Tana's hand went to her mouth. She rose and limped back toward the ranch house.

"Way to go, Curtis," Fort muttered to himself. He was tempted to follow Tana. Instead, he sat on a rock and stared at the ground in front of him. His throat was dry, and when he blinked his eyes felt like sandpaper. His aching arms and legs felt stiff and heavy.

He gritted his teeth as he thought about his dad, Billy, and Mrs. Newton. They all needed medical attention right now. He hoped his mom was okay, but knew she must be worried sick about her family. He felt like screaming, but Tana and the younger boys might hear him. For a moment he considered running away—just disappearing, but he knew he couldn't do that to those who needed him. Besides, where would he go?

Suddenly, the ground in front of Fort grew bright. A shaft of sunlight beaming through gray clouds warmed him. An arc of color glimmered between the clouds and the earth —part of a rainbow. Taking a deep breath, he wiped the tears from his cheeks.

He stood up and studied the flooded creek again. Even if the water were calm, he might have difficulty swimming the width of the flooded creek. The current, with its unpredictable undertows, could be a deadly threat for the best of swimmers. Even with a life jacket and a canoe it would be dangerous, and he didn't have either.

Fort heard a sound that made him turn—the caw of a lone crow. He watched the bird as it flew over the tree-lined creek. Within minutes, Fort realized with envy, the crow would be able to see the highway to the south.

He refocused his attention on a narrow section of the creek about a quarter of a mile upstream. There the steam narrowed where it sliced between two steep, rocky banks. A flicker of hope stirred within him.

He gazed back toward the dark smoke rising from the bonfire. His growling stomach reminded him of the chickens still cooking. His mouth watered as he headed back to the ranch.

Fort was pleased to see that the boys had washed his knife and some dishes in the bucket of hot water and set them out to dry in the sun, as he had instructed them. So many things had already gone wrong in the last twenty-four hours. He didn't want to add food poisoning to the list.

The skin of the broiling chicken was now golden

brown, its juices sputtering and hissing as they dripped onto the hot coals.

"Looks like you've done a good job of turning the chicken so the meat has cooked evenly," he said to the Scouts. "Shall we give it a try?"

The boys beamed proudly as Fort grabbed hold of the skewer and lifted.

"Ow!" The stick was too hot to hold, and he dropped it back between the tire rims. He shook his stinging hand before sticking a singed finger into his mouth.

He saw an old towel lying in the mud and shook it until most of the dirt came off, then used it to protect his hands as he lifted the broiling meat. He carefully placed the chicken on a plate and sliced into the breast. The fresh white meat was steaming all the way to the bone. Holding one end of the skewer up, he used his knife to slide the chicken off the stick.

He returned to the fire and tapped the mud-covered chicken with the stick. The mud had dried and hardened in the heat. He began to push the clay ball away from the coals, but stopped when the clay split.

Fearing that the meat would get dirty, Fort tossed the stick aside and used the towel to scoop the dried mud-ball out of the coals. He placed the contents of the towel on a plate near the broiled chicken. With his pocketknife and burning fingers, he carefully pried open the hardened mud.

The chicken's skin stuck to the baked mud and peeled away from the meat. Fort sampled a piece of breast meat to make sure it was cooked, closing his eyes as he savored the taste.

Remembering that he needed to leave soon, Fort quickly sawed, pulled, and cut, until both chickens were piles of steaming meat. The air filled with the smell of freshly cooked poultry.

He handed a plateful of chicken down to Tana in the basement, as the eleven-year-olds attacked the meat like a school of piranha. Fort grabbed a golden-brown drumstick from the broiled chicken and bit into it. The skin was crispy and had a strong charcoal flavor. He noticed just a hint of another, less pleasant, taste. Burnt rubber. Oh well, he thought, nothing's perfect.

An hour later Fort stood at the top of the steep creek bank. Wiping his greasy mouth on his forearm, he could still taste the meal that he and Tana and the other boys had devoured. As they had nibbled the bones clean, Fort had explained his plan.

At first Tana had protested that it was too

dangerous, but Fort had convinced her that he knew what he was doing. Then Tana and the boys had wanted to go with him, or at least watch him cross the creek. But Fort had been firm—their job was to look after Mrs. Newton and to keep the fire burning.

Fort didn't tell them that he didn't want them to see him drown if he failed—or even worse, to drown themselves trying to rescue him. Deep inside he also feared that he might not have the guts to do it.

He had searched the ranch site for equipment he could use and then had left Tana in charge. The items he had salvaged now lay at his feet. He cut the plugs off each end of a fifty-foot electrical extension cord.

Next, he selected a foot-wide piece of metal that resembled a boat anchor. Its base was V-shaped and sharpened on the outside edges. A stem extended diagonally upward from the center of the V, with square holes drilled near the top of the stem. Fort had seen dozens of these attached to an implement his grandfather used to till farmland. He knew it was a chisel sweep, but today it would be his grappling hook.

He threaded one end of the bright-orange extension cord through the chisel holes that normally held bolts, and tied a knot to secure it. He carefully looped the rest of the cord around his elbow and the palm of his hand.

Slipping the coiled cord off his arm, he held it loosely in his left hand. With his right hand, Fort picked up the line nearest his grappling hook and swung it up, then let it fall in a circle to his side. He twirled the hook with increasing speed as he targeted a sturdy tree branch on the other side of the roaring creek. He swung the hook with a burst of power and let it fly.

The hook and cord sailed high above him before plunging into the angry current. Yanking the cord back, he re-coiled it, and then hurled the chisel sweep again. This time the hook crashed into the branches of the tree and dropped to the rocky ground below.

He reeled in the cord and hurled the grappling hook again and again. Time after time it fell, useless, to the ground or the turbulent water below. Fort growled in frustration.

Taking a deep breath, he focused intensely on the targeted limb and visualized exactly what he wanted to happen. This time the hook sailed over the limb, caught on it, and swung gracefully a few feet above the ground. He gently pulled on the orange cord and watched as the hook inched upward toward the stout branch. Holding his breath, he slowly eased the hook into the tree limb. Success! The V-shaped metal piece wedged itself firmly between two branches.

He pulled with increasing strength to test its hold

and hooted aloud when the hook held tight. Then, eyeing the raging current below, he looped the cord around his hips and leaned back, adding his weight to the strength in his arms and legs. Still the hook held fast in the tree limb across the creek.

Fort tied the loose end of the orange cord around his waist. Turning to a sturdy oak tree, he reached up and grabbed a hefty limb, then climbed halfway up the oak, about ten feet higher than the grappling hook across the creek.

He untied the knot at his waist and looped the extension cord around the tree trunk. He drew the slack out of the line and quickly tied a taut-line hitch in the cord. Slipping the knot farther away from the tree trunk, he tightened the cord as he pulled. He let the line hang momentarily, knowing the slipknot would hold until he loosened it. He felt a little slackness in the cord, so he tugged on the knot again until the cord was as tight as he could stretch it. Now he had a strong line stretched firmly from his side of the creek down to the tree on the other side.

Fort viewed his work with satisfaction, but the angry rumble of the floodwater below reminded him of the danger he would soon face. Suddenly dizzy, he climbed back down the tree. His feet touched the soil, his legs buckled, and he crumpled to the ground. He couldn't move.

I really don't have to do this, he told himself. He could go back to the ranch house and just wait for help to arrive. Besides, that's what he had been taught. "Place your signals and wait for help. Don't get yourself into deeper trouble." His training had also taught him he shouldn't take such a risk alone. He should have at least one buddy—preferably three—with him. Also, he didn't have a life jacket.

He knew if his dad or mom were here, they wouldn't let him do this. They would say it was too dangerous. He should figure out another way, even if it took days to get help. But that's the problem, he thought. Dad needs medical help right now, or he might die. Mrs. Newton needs help now, or she could be paralyzed. Billy needs a doctor. I can't just wait and let them all suffer.

I'm going to do it! he thought. He didn't dare swim the flooded stream, even with a log to help him stay afloat. The current would sweep him downstream much faster than he could swim across, and he didn't know what hazards might await him farther downstream. This way he could simply zip across the creek on the orange extension cord.

Years ago, he remembered, he and his little brothers had rigged a small zip line in their backyard. It had worked well until the rope finally rotted and broke. The big difference, he realized, was that today he would have to be successful on his first try. The cord or limb could break, a knot could fail, or the hook could slip. If so, he would plunge into the worst part of the raging floodwater.

He recalled seeing TV news pictures showing police and firemen dragging the bottom of rivers trying to find the body of a drowning victim. Even worse, thought Fort, they might never find him. His body would bloat and rot and then be eaten by fish or wild animals—or maggots. The thought made his stomach turn, and a sour taste rose in his mouth.

Fort rose on his hands and knees as the contents of his stomach surged up his throat and out onto the grass in front of him. He heaved again and again, even after he had nothing left to vomit. Spitting and wiping the sour bile from his lips, he sat back, arms wrapped around his knees. For a moment he let the gentle breeze cool his face. Then he climbed to his feet.

No other way is possible, and no one can do this but me, Fort reasoned. I can do it. He visualized himself sailing across the floodwaters and dropping off the zip line onto the other bank. Then, by hiking southward an hour or two to the highway, he could have help on the way. His decision made, he felt better.

Fort picked up the last piece of his scavenged equipment, a rusty bicycle chain, slipped it under his belt, and climbed back up the tree. Once he reached the bright-orange cord, he tested the knot and stretched the cord tight again. He studied the grappling hook, checking it one last time.

He pulled the bicycle chain from under his belt, draped it over the extension cord, and gripped the ends of the chain tightly in each hand. Then he bent his knees slightly and leaned toward the flooding creek.

Fort flinched at a loud noise below him. Butch stood at the base of the tree, clawing the trunk with his paws as he barked a greeting and tried to climb up to Fort.

In a fraction of a second, Fort's thoughts turned from alarm that the dog was loose to fear as he realized he had lost his balance. He pulled hard on the bicycle chain to right himself on the tree limb, but it was too late. He was already leaning too far away from the tree.

His body twisted sideways as he slipped, and he swung off the tree limb into mid-air.

CHAPTER
TEN

Clinging to the bicycle chain, Fort wrenched to the side, then twisted forward as he streaked down the orange line. The floodwaters seemed to reach up toward him. In a blur, he zipped across the stream, the rocky riverbank rushing toward him. Too late, he realized he had underestimated the stretch in the electrical cord. Instead of heading for the top of the rocks, he was speeding straight into them.

He squeezed his eyes shut an instant before slamming into the rocks. The impact forced the breath from his lungs, and the bicycle chain slipped from his hands. He grasped, in vain, for a handhold. Outcroppings of sharp-edged limestone raked his face, arms, and body as he slid downward.

He landed in the raging creek. The momentum of his slide plunged him underwater, and then cold, frothy-brown water whisked him downstream. He held his breath as the dark torrent rolled him in crazy, awkward somersaults. Arms and legs thrashing, he fought to find the surface.

In darkness, his face slammed into the creek bed.

His nose and one cheek scraped across a jagged rock before the rushing water propelled him onward. A submerged boulder hammered his right leg, and pain shot through his knee. His eyes opened briefly to gritty blackness, and his lungs burned for fresh air. He covered his head with his hands, tucking his knees and elbows against his chest. A human ball, he tumbled helplessly with the current.

His face suddenly broke through the water's surface. Gasping for breath, his arms and legs thrashing, he coughed and spat water. Sucking in air, he coughed again. Twirling in slow circles as he glided downstream, through a fog of dizziness, he could alternately see the blue sky, the tree-lined creek bank, and the frothy floodwater.

He stopped thrashing and calmed himself, then rolled onto his back, took a slow, deep breath, and arched his chest. He let his arms and legs go limp as he forced himself to relax and breathe normally. Eyes closed, he felt his confidence begin to return. He had almost drowned, he knew, but now he would be okay. He could float on his back for hours.

Feeling some strength return to his body, he calmly rolled onto his belly, looked around, and laughed aloud. This isn't so bad. After his close call he now felt wonderfully alive, full of energy. Floating at the brisk pace of the flood was exhilarating. Maybe he had overestimated the danger. Instead of rigging the zip line, maybe he should have just waded into the flood to swim across.

Looking toward the left bank, he began a gentle dog paddle. Pain stabbed through his right knee, so he carefully stretched out his right leg and switched to a sidestroke, letting his left arm and leg do the work. He remembered that he shouldn't swim straight toward the bank. The exertion would just wear him out. Letting the current carry him forward, and swimming with regular, relaxed strokes, he made good progress toward the creek bank.

From the corner of his eye, Fort noticed motion on the right shoreline. Butch was bounding through waist-high weeds on the stream bank. The big dog jumped onto a fallen tree trunk and stood, barking in Fort's direction. The thought of the dog running loose worried him, but at the same time he was pleased to have Butch along for company, at least for a while.

The flood carried Fort around a sharp, narrow curve. Ahead, he could see a huge tree lying across the creek. A mammoth-sized ball of brown earth anchored the uprooted cottonwood to the creek bank. Leaves fluttered and branches shuddered as the current surged under the doomed timber.

Fort pictured himself being sucked under the tree and drowned, entangled in its submerged branches. He stroked and kicked toward the creek bank, but pain seared through his right leg as his knee tightened, then refused to bend. The current quickly carried him into the branches. Grabbing a leaf-covered limb, he pulled himself up. The branch bent, then snapped, and Fort slipped back into the frothy current.

He reached for a thicker branch and pulled again. The current dragged his legs down and ahead of him. The rushing water sucked his body under the massive tree trunk. Rough cottonwood bark scraped Fort's belly as he pulled one last time with all his strength. The branch he was holding bent more and more, dunking his neck and shoulders into the water. He grabbed a thick tree limb with both hands.

Knowing he could do twenty pull-ups in the weight room at school, he clenched his jaw and pulled, but the rushing water dragged him downward. His face dipped into the water. Coughing and spitting, he tasted earthy, grit-filled fluid.

He pulled harder, his arms trembling, but rushing water edged up over his cheeks, then his eyes. Holding his breath, he pulled again as the water tugged relentlessly and the muscles in his hand cramped with fatigue. His fingers trembled, then loosened. One hand slipped from the branch, and the other was wrenched loose.

Fort's cheek ground across rough bark as he was dragged farther under the partly submerged tree. Muddy water filled his nose before he could hold his breath. He sensed his legs starting to rise on the other side of the tree trunk as his head passed under the bottom. Branches and leaves raked his body and face. He could feel one leg scrape along a branch as he was dragged away. Then his foot slipped into a fork of the branches and wedged tight.

Lungs screaming for fresh air, Fort kicked frantically. The foot wouldn't budge. Bending double against the powerful flood, he reached for his shoe, and then twisted his foot from side to side until the shoe was loose. He yanked his foot free. Plunging onward through submerged branches, he clawed his way back to the frothy surface and took great gulping breaths of air.

He calmed himself as he floated onward in the rapidly moving current. His breathing returned to normal. The floodwater was littered with driftwood floating at the same speed as Fort. A log the size of a fence post bobbed in front of him, and he pushed the slippery timber aside.

Close to the right bank, he noticed a smaller piece

of driftwood that seemed to move by itself in the slower current near the shore. He studied it more closely and realized it was an animal swimming, its body submerged, but its nose out of the water. Fort saw black fur and a white stripe.

Glancing from side to side, he saw that he was too far from either creek bank to reach one quickly. He looked back toward the skunk and could see the animal's pointed face with ink-black eyes on either side of a snow-white stripe. It was moving toward him—fast. Fort could feel his heart pounding.

It's probably harmless, he figured, just trying to get across the flooded creek. He hoped it would just ignore him and continue its journey across the creek. The skunk grew bigger in Fort's view, heading straight for him.

Even though it was many yards away, Fort splashed the water and yelled. The skunk kept coming. Fort grabbed a floating stick, tossed it toward the animal, and then shouted and thrashed the water. The sleek beast stopped briefly, raised its head slightly, and turned back toward the right bank. Soon it was on the muddy bank, where it waddled a few steps away from the water, then shook itself, spraying water in all directions.

Fort was drifting well past the skunk when he

heard an angry snarl and loud barking. Looking back he saw Butch charge at the skunk. A black-and-white plume rose, then dipped, just before the Rottweiler bowled it over. Then both animals were lost in a whirlwind of action. The relative quiet of the creek bank was ripped apart by Butch's frantic growls mixed with the shrill squeal of the smaller animal.

Fort couldn't see how the skunk could possibly survive the big dog's furious attack, but Butch's angry growl was replaced with a yelp of pain as he spun in a circle, rolled on the ground, and pawed at his face. The skunk disappeared into the bushes. The dog's cries grew more distant as the floodwaters carried Fort farther downstream. He hoped Butch would be okay.

Fort eyed the water around him, just to be sure there weren't any more surprises. He started to breathe a little more easily and to concentrate on getting across the creek. Ahead, the stream was wider and ran more slowly. He swam toward the left bank.

Between strokes he could see a sharp turn in the watercourse, with steep banks. Difficult to climb, he realized, especially with an injured leg. He doubted that he could reach the shoreline before he was carried around the turn. Seeing a floating log, Fort paddled to it and grabbed hold, then draped his arms and chest across the driftwood, welcoming the chance to rest.

Watching the creek bank grow even steeper as he continued his speedy ride, he hoped for a wider, slower stretch of water ahead. Instead, the creek became narrower, and the water grew more turbulent, hurling Fort around the curve with increasing speed. He hardly noticed the deep rumble at first, but it grew louder as he was whipped around the bend in the stream.

Just ahead, the creek was partially blocked by two huge columns of cement. The floodwater roared in a frothy torrent as it funneled between massive bridge supports and then rushed into a churning whirlpool. Fort was carried between the skeletal jaws of the washed-out bridge.

Struggling to get a better hold, he wrapped his arms and legs tightly around the log as he shot between the cement columns. He caught a glimpse of blue sky just before he plunged into a roaring cauldron of angry brown water.

The torrent rolled him over and over. His eyes shut, he waited for a painful impact with rock or wood in the cold, wet darkness. Totally disoriented, he was surprised to feel warmth on his face. He opened his eyes to find himself at the surface just as the undertow dragged him down again.

Fort clasped the driftwood to his chest as he somersaulted through the churning current. He feared he would soon lose consciousness and suck in a deadly breath of water. His lungs demanded air, even if he had to inhale water.

Suddenly he felt air on his bare arms and face. Opening his eyes, he saw that the log had popped back to the surface, and he was floating downstream again. He flopped on top of the driftwood and gasped, letting the current carry him as he rested.

Clutching the driftwood, he forced himself to stroke with one arm, then kick with his left leg. Keeping a wary eye downstream, he paddled to the shoreline. Once there, he crawled up the muddy, weed-covered bank and collapsed.

CHAPTER
ELEVEN

Spring sunshine warmed Fort as he lay on his back. Wildflowers perfumed the air. A gentle breeze whispered through the leaves around him, as a meadowlark sang in the distance. Fort saw Tana Newton lean over and kiss his cheek, her silky-brown hair caressing his face. The vision shimmered, then faded away as he slowly awakened. His right knee throbbed, and he ached all over. Blocking out the pain, he tried to recall the pleasant dream. He could still feel the warm sun and hear the songbird. The scent of wildflowers was still there, but seemed a little strong. Fort coughed as the smell overwhelmed his senses. Where is Tana? he wondered.

When Fort opened his eyes, he saw brown eyes and long lashes. The truth jolted him. Tana hadn't kissed his cheek, and Tana's hair had not caressed his face. He was gazing into the big, brown eyes of the Rottweiler. Fort sprang to his feet, and Butch leaped back.

Fort coughed again, waving his hand in front of his face. Butch reeked, and not from wildflowers.

Remembering Butch's encounter with the skunk, Fort wondered how the dog had crossed the floodwaters. Butch panted with his head hung low as water dripped from his matted hair.

"You crossed the creek like I did, didn't you?" asked Fort. "The hard way." He was touched that the dog had followed him. At least he seemed to be okay, and the stench would fade—eventually.

Anxious to be on his way, he snatched up a sturdy shaft of driftwood to use as a walking stick, then hobbled farther up the bank. He continued uphill to a rocky ledge that extended around the winding creek bank in both directions. Seeing no easy way around the outcropping, he tossed his stick ahead of him and climbed over the ledge. He paused to catch his breath, hoping the remainder of the walk would be easier.

From behind him came a buzzing rattle, and a large snake shot toward his right leg. Fangs stabbed through his pants and clamped into his calf. Almost instantly the snake opened its jaws and attempted to retreat, but its fangs caught in the denim pant leg. The snake twisted and recoiled as if to strike again.

Fort grabbed the snake behind its head. As he pulled, the snake's body wrapped around his leg and tightened like a tourniquet. Fort shrieked and yanked until the needle-sharp fangs tore out of the denim pant leg. He pulled until the scaly coil around his leg loosened and sprang free, then he staggered to his feet as the rattler's body slithered around his arm. The buzzing rattle whipped across Fort's cheek. Grasping the snake's body with his free hand, Fort pulled, slowly and steadily, until he uncoiled the snake from his arm.

He had the rattler stretched out before him when he heard a growl and a bark. Suddenly, Butch was in front of him, jaws clenched on the body of the snake, trying to drag it away.

For a moment Fort considered releasing the snake and letting the dog have it. Then he remembered Butch's encounter with the skunk. The dog was unlikely to get away from the rattler with just a bad smell. Still holding one end of the snake in each hand, he lifted the rattler waist high as the dog growled and tugged at it.

"No, Butch!" he commanded. The dog ignored him. Fort lifted the snake a little higher and kicked Butch in the ribs. The dog yelped and cowered away. Stepping toward the rock ledge, Fort heaved the rattler toward the swollen creek. He watched the snake sail upward, then writhe in mid-air before plunging into the floodwaters.

Fort picked up his walking stick and ran, not stopping until he was well away from the creek.

Spotting a bare patch of ground, he searched it quickly for snakes, and then dropped down on it. Heart racing, he pulled up his pant leg and studied the bite. Two puncture marks and a U-shaped bruise showed where the rattler's jaw had clamped into him. He shuddered and groaned.

"Stupid! Stupid! Stupid!" he yelled, knowing that rattlers were native to the area and that rocky outcroppings were favorite places for them to bask in the sun. He pounded the ground with a clenched fist until he was out of breath.

Regaining his composure, he shook his head and tried to remember first aid for snakebite. "Don't cut the wound open and try to suck out the poison as they used to recommend," he recalled one instructor saying. "That causes more harm than good. Don't use a tourniquet. Treat a snakebite like any other puncture wound. Clean it and bandage it. The victim should rest and try to position the bite below the heart so the poison doesn't spread so quickly. Get medical attention promptly."

That's just great, thought Fort. I don't even have a Band-Aid, much less a first-aid kit. He thought about his father and the others waiting for him to bring help. Rest wasn't an option at this point. He tried to remember if rattlesnake bites were really fatal. The old western movies usually showed the victims dying gruesome, painful deaths, but how much of that was really true? He wasn't sure.

He thought back to his decision to cross the flooded creek, even if it killed him. Well, this might do it. Butch nuzzled Fort. The big dog's thick tongue slurped across his face. "Phew!" Fort coughed. "You stink." He pushed the hound aside. Butch wagged his tail and bounded around him eagerly.

After a few minutes Fort stood up, leaned on his walking stick, and gazed around. Gently rolling, grass-covered hills lay before him and to either side. He saw no sign of humanity anywhere, not even the black plume of smoke from the burning tire. He reached into his pocket for his compass, but it was gone. Probably tumbled out in the creek.

Tired, bruised, and still jittery, Fort cried out in frustration. He yearned to be home, to sleep, and to see his mom. Now he was snake bitten, dog bitten, and lost. Banging the walking stick on his forehead, he gritted his teeth. Then he swung the stick in an arc and pounded it into the ground. Enraged and fighting back tears, he slammed it into the earth again and again. Finally, he slumped back down on the ground.

Sighing, he tried to remember his training for the Wilderness Survival merit badge. "If you get lost," he recalled aloud, "just remember to 'STOP.' 'S' is for sit. 'T' is for think. 'O' is for observe. 'P' is for plan."

As he sat in the grass, he started to think through his situation. The creek flowed to the south and west, but it had many twists and turns along the way, so it was not a reliable indicator of direction. He needed to know which way was south, or he might walk for hours in the wrong direction.

Looking up, he shaded his eyes. Most of the clouds were gone now, and the sun was almost directly overhead, not clearly indicating which direction was east or west.

Suddenly he remembered what he should do. He picked up a dried weed stalk, broke off a foot-long piece, and jammed it into the wet soil. Carefully, he positioned the stick so the tip pointed directly at the sun, leaving no shadow.

Feeling more confident, he lay back in the grass and closed his eyes. Better to rest a few minutes now than to waste time walking in the wrong direction.

After a while he sat up. He felt dizzy, his stomach churned, his mouth was dry, and the angry snakebite throbbed. He staggered to his feet, careful not to dislodge the little stick in the ground, and then he smiled. A thin finger of a shadow pointed away from the marker.

As the earth rotates on its axis, he knew, the sun appears to move from east to west. As long as the stick pointed directly at the sun, there would be no shadow. But after a few minutes, the sun had moved across the sky just enough to create a tiny shadow at the base of the rod. As the sun moved farther west, the lengthening shadow pointed to the east.

Fort grabbed his driftwood walking stick to steady himself. The world seemed to be spinning around him, and he felt like throwing up, but he forced himself to focus on the little shadow. He turned until his left shoulder pointed to the east. Then, raising his eyes to the horizon, he knew he was looking south. In the distance he could see three cottonwood trees clumped closely together. Those trees would be his landmarks. As long as he walked toward them, he would be heading south. He set off in search of the highway.

The hike up the grass-covered slope seemed endless. His swelling right calf throbbed with pain. Each awkward hobble with his walking stick sent needles of fire through his right knee and leg, but he plodded ahead, his eyes fixed on the clump of trees in the distance. When he had left the disastrous campsite, it had been midmorning. Now, glancing toward the sun, he estimated it to be mid-afternoon.

Picking up the pace, he prayed that he wasn't already too late to help his father and the others.

As Fort swung his walking stick forward, a clump of grass seemed to explode with life. His heart surged as something streaked away. Butch barked and raced after it. Fort exhaled with relief as he watched the dog chase a cottontail rabbit across the prairie and out of sight around a hill.

Finally he reached the hilltop. The gradual down-slope in front of him was overgrown with brush and small trees. Farther out, he could see miles of rolling pasture crisscrossed with barbed-wire fence. No highway was visible. Wondering how he could have been so wrong, he felt hopelessness creep over him. He didn't know what to do next.

Then he saw it—a big eighteen-wheeler seemed to speed across the prairie. Fort was close enough to recognize a "possum belly" double-decked cattle trailer, but the highway itself, no more than a quarter of a mile away, was hidden from view by sprawling brush.

With tears of relief, he shambled toward the road. His walking stick kept catching on clumps of grass and on the low-lying branches of scrub oak and cedar trees. Stepping out of the patch of brush, he could see the blacktop of the asphalt highway, each side lined with a barbed-wire fence. A red car flashed by on the highway. The road was only a couple of hundred feet in front of him.

He heard something snort behind him and turned. A herd of half-grown steers of various breeds looked placidly toward Fort for a moment, then returned to their grazing.

As he lurched toward the highway, he could feel the snake venom continuing its work on him. Sweat beaded on his forehead as the rest of his body shivered with chills.

Halfway to the highway, the grass thinned to a shallow, rock-strewn gully. Butch suddenly appeared, panting, with his tail wagging. Fort caught a whiff of skunk and limped onward across the rocks.

He was nearly across the gully when he heard another sound. One of the cattle trotted toward him. With its head high and tail raised, it glared and snorted. Fort could see a full scrotum dangling between its hind legs. A bull.

The half-grown, black bull had foot-long horns and a slight hump above its shoulders. Fort remembered the year his grandfather had bought some cattle that were part Brahma. The hump-shouldered calves had acted so wildly that his grandpa had vowed to never buy that breed again.

The other animals approached rapidly. Within seconds Fort faced a dozen agitated cattle. His mind raced. Apparently the sight of the Rottweiler had annoyed the young bull, and its snorts of alarm had excited the rest of the herd into action.

The bull charged several feet toward Butch, then stopped and snorted. Fort took a step back toward the highway. Several of the steers responded to his motion by charging a few feet toward him. Fort staggered back another step. His foot caught on the walking stick, and he toppled to the rocky ground. The cattle quickly surrounded Fort and Butch. Fort imagined the steers goring and stomping them into a bloody pile of flesh.

Instantly, he forgot the pain wracking his body and the poison in his blood. His mind cleared, his muscles pumped full strength, and his body was filled with energizing adrenaline. He scrambled to his feet, swung the stick high over his head, and screamed. The animals snorted and backed away a few feet. He grabbed a baseball-sized rock from the ground and hurled it at the nearest steer. The rock bounced off the animal's shoulder, and the steer flinched and jumped back.

Fort heaved stone after stone. A rock hit one of the steers on its nose. The animal shook its head and trotted away from the herd. Several of the others followed quickly. Fort continued his barrage of rocks as more of the steers turned and fled. Finally, only the young hump-shouldered bull remained.

It lowered its head and charged toward Butch. The dog scrambled to Fort's side, and the beast rushed past him. The black bull turned and charged back. Its rock-hard head rammed Fort backwards, and a horn sliced across his ribs as he slipped to the ground. Hooves pounded the rough terrain as the bull sped past.

Fort lay stunned. The world seemed to spin as he watched the bull lurch sideways, its hooves stomping. Fort hoped that if he lay still, the bull would lose interest and leave him alone. Instead, the bull charged, horns lowered. The impact of the Brahma's head knocked Fort across the rocky ground. He rolled onto his side and then tried to stand.

A staccato series of savage barks ripped the air. Butch rushed at the bull's hindquarters. The dog's head wrenched from side to side as his powerful jaws ripped and tore. The bull bellowed and swung its head back, knocking Butch over, then pinning him to the earth with a stout horn. Butch yelped, then lay motionless.

The bull spun away from the dog, paused momentarily, and then charged Fort. A horn hooked under Fort's chest, and he felt himself being hurled upward. Tumbling in midair above the bull, Fort saw the blue sky, then the brown earth racing to meet him. As he hit the ground, a lightning bolt of pain shot though his body.

Numb with pain, he couldn't move. His mind swirled with confusion as he stared dully at the sky, only vaguely aware of the bloody dog lying next to him. Fort knew the bull would kill both of them if it continued its attack.

Even through the fog clouding his mind, he realized that he had failed. Picturing his father in a coma, Billy holding a broken arm, and Mrs. Newton lying helpless on the basement floor, Fort knew he had let them all down. He felt himself slipping toward unconsciousness.

Butch whined. The bull snorted, pawed the ground, and lowered its head. Fort's forehead throbbed, and his blood began to boil. He gritted his teeth and grunted. Then, realizing he was losing control, he stopped himself. Imagining his blood cooling, he felt himself grow calm. He imagined his blood turning ice cold as he filled himself with resolve.

He dragged himself to his feet as the hump-shouldered bull charged toward Butch. Fort saw a bloody stone lying next to Butch, scooped it off the ground and threw it across the bull's path. The bull veered away from Butch and hooked a horn at the stone as Fort turned to run for the fence. His legs wobbled as he staggered forward.

A horn knocked Fort's feet out from under him. He toppled over the animal's neck, grabbing a horn as he fell. The animal snorted and charged forward. A horn in each hand, Fort dragged himself along beside the bull's hot, steamy neck.

Blood rushed to Fort's head, and his jaw clenched. Forcing his rage back, he imagined what he must do. He had seen it done in rodeos, and now it might be his only chance. Hands still gripping the horns, he pulled his legs off the ground, tucking them against his chest as the bull raced ahead. With the full weight of Fort's body now on the left side of its head, the young bull slowed to an awkward walk.

Muscles straining, Fort pushed down on the bull's left horn while pulling up on the right. The young bull stumbled to its knees. Using the forward momentum of the bull's stumble, Fort continued to twist the beast's horns until its head was turned almost upside down, snout upward. The half-grown animal rolled onto its back, its legs pawing the air.

Fort lay on his side, a horn firmly in each hand as he twisted the bull's head. The animal kicked and rolled in an effort to stand up, but it was pinned. With leverage in his favor, Fort knew he could hold the beast down as long as he needed to. Lying in the grass next to the bull, he heaved great gulps of air, trying to catch his breath as he decided what to do next.

At rodeos he had watched cowboys leap from their horses in the bulldog events and pin steers just as he had done. Then the cowboy would simply stand up and step back. The animal would scramble to its feet, shake its head, and trot away. But this isn't a rodeo, thought Fort. And there's no cowboy on a horse or rodeo clown to rescue me if the bull decides to charge again.

He gazed into the black eyes of the bull. It was just an animal, neither good nor evil, but with a temper. He could hear it breathing heavily, its tongue hanging out of its mouth. The beast's thick, foamy saliva flowed over Fort's hand before dripping to the ground. The bull's legs had stopped thrashing.

Time to find out if it's had enough. Releasing the animal's horns, Fort stood up and moved backward on shaky legs. The bull rolled to its belly, tucked its legs under its body, then wobbled to its feet. Fort raised his arms wide and growled like a bear.

The bull lowered its head, stepped back, and snorted. Fort's heart nearly stopped. He knew he didn't have the strength to run or jump out of the way. The young bull snorted again. It shook its head, took another step back, then trotted across the pasture and disappeared into the brush.

Fort stared blankly at the thicket for a moment, breathing hard. Pain seared his ribs with each breath. His head throbbed, his mouth was parched, his body burned with feverish heat, and his stomach turned with nausea. He shifted his feet, and pain stabbed through his right knee and leg.

After wiping his face with a trembling hand, he stared at the mixture of blood and dirty sweat covering his fingers. Dazed, he couldn't recall getting cut. He looked down at himself. His shirt and pants were torn, bloody, and filthy.

Hearing a meadowlark sing in the distance, Fort looked up. He felt the world dancing slowly around him and saw the sky shimmering blue. The air was heavy with the scent of sage, and a crisp breeze cooled the back of his neck. From behind him came a metallic clink that made him jump. He gasped in pain at the sudden movement, but when he saw the source of the noise, he felt overwhelming joy. A car and a farm truck had stopped on the highway. The drivers were getting out of their vehicles and hurrying toward him.

Fort struggled back to Butch's limp body. Stooping next to the Rottweiler, he brushed his hand across the dog's shoulder. Butch's eyes flickered open, and he whined. Fort gently scooped his hands under Butch to lift him. Instead, the dog squirmed, then scrambled to his feet.

Fort wobbled toward the fence with Butch limping after him. A Kansas Highway Patrol car pulled up behind the other vehicles. Fort's eyes began to water, his throat tightened, and his lips quivered as he fought back the tears.

CHAPTER
TWELVE

Fort squirmed on a metal folding chair in the cavernous rotunda of the Kansas State Capitol. The air carried the smell of government buildings: a mixture of dust and cleaning fluids. Goosebumps prickled his skin, just as they had when he saw the copper-plated dome over the Topeka skyline.

This was the heart of democracy, where elected representatives from one hundred and five counties gathered to chart the future of the state. He remembered that he would turn eighteen in less than a year and looked forward to voting for the first time.

Elevated on a foot-high riser, he gazed out over dozens of people seated in crowded rows. Television cameramen, photographers, and reporters ringed the room, chatting casually among themselves.

Fort studied the colorful mural that dominated the wall across from him. John Brown, the bearded antislavery firebrand, raised a rifle in anger. The scene recalled the state's bloody struggle with the slavery issue before the Civil War, and Fort was struck by the intensity of Brown's dark glare.

The eyes seemed to meet Fort's gaze, and he felt

the fanatic reach out to him. He looked away as a chill ran through him. Realizing his imagination had played a trick, he glanced around the room, hoping no one had noticed his moment of discomfort.

He forced himself to look at the painting again, but avoided the penetrating eyes. Dark clouds in the picture reminded him of the Scouts' tornado-stricken campout nearly a year earlier. After he had reached the road, the highway patrolman had listened to his story, asked a few questions, and then radioed for help. Two National Guard helicopters were diverted from rescue work in Strickler and soon spotted the Scouts' signal fires. In less than two hours, everybody had been evacuated to the nearest hospital.

Fort crossed his legs, pulled back his right pant leg, and scratched the skin over his calf muscle. Between the curly brown hairs, he still bore two pea-sized red scars from the rattlesnake's bite.

Rubbing his hand across the faded wound, he remembered that the patrolman had rushed him across the county for his first dose of antivenin. After spending the next several days in an intensive care unit, he had begun weeks of physical therapy to regain full use of his leg. The little scars would always remind him of that weekend.

Glancing at the audience in front of him, he

spotted Mrs. Newton in a wheelchair. Surgery had repaired the damage to her back, and the doctors predicted that with therapy she would walk normally again.

Fort's mom sat with the other parents. Seeing her reminded him of his relief when he had learned she was safe and uninjured. At the first sound of the warning sirens, she had hurried to the basement. Moments later, their house was gone.

Fort's father, sitting next to him, had awakened from his coma the next day. He had recovered quickly enough to attend Mr. Crawford's funeral. Several other men sat next to Fort and his dad. Like Fort, they wore Scout uniforms.

He could see Billy talking and laughing with the other Scouts. Billy's arm had healed completely. Fort had apologized to the little boy again soon after the campout and had had a long visit with Billy's parents. He had offered to plead guilty if they decided to have him arrested for hurting Billy. They all met with the county attorney and agreed that, if Fort kept his temper under control, he would not be prosecuted.

He realized now that the campout had been a turning point for him. Over the last year he had learned to control his temper. The local newspapers had featured him in a story about the tragic outing. Almost immediately he had begun receiving requests to speak at schools and various youth groups.

Not feeling comfortable talking about his own heroism, Fort had focused his speeches on how the incident helped him solve the problem of his temper. Now he regularly received letters from kids, and even a few adults, telling him how they too had changed their lives for the better.

Chairs squeaked on the marble floor. The audience stood and applauded as the state's popular young governor entered the room. The tall, blond-haired man smiled and worked his way around the room, shaking outstretched hands.

Fort's insides began to ache. As he had done many times in the last year, he imagined that he could control the temperature of his own blood, and then intentionally cooled it until his nervousness was under control.

He caught Tana Newton's attention. His spine tingled when she smiled. She had taken to wearing western-style clothes almost everywhere. Today she had on a white blouse with a cowboy pattern of yokes and swirls. Around her neck hung the turquoise necklace he had given her for Christmas.

Tana's horse, Brandy, had been found unhurt after the tornado, grazing in a nearby pasture. Even though

Fort had still been weak from his injuries, he had gone to the rodeo the next weekend to watch Tana and the palomino compete in the barrel race. Since then Fort and Tana had been to many rodeos together. This year Tana and Brandy were contenders for the state championship.

Fort could see Tana beam as the governor approached to shake her hand. She leaned close to the man and whispered. Smiling, he glanced toward Fort, then turned back to Tana and nodded. The governor approached the riser, greeted Fort and the uniformed adults, and stepped behind the podium.

"Ladies and gentlemen," the governor began in his familiar, crisp voice, "as an eleven-year-old, I joined the Boy Scouts looking for fun and adventure. I wasn't disappointed. My friends and I hiked, fished, and canoed on our monthly campouts for many years. Fun and adventure were only part of what I gained while a Boy Scout. As I completed the various requirements to become an Eagle Scout, I learned teamwork and shared leadership, problem solving, and persistence. As your governor, I try to use these skills every day."

Suddenly it occurred to Fort that he might be governor himself some day. No way! he thought. Then he reconsidered. Why not? If I prepare myself, with a little luck, anything is possible.

Fort's attention shifted back to the governor's speech.

"The Boy Scout motto is 'Be Prepared,'" continued the governor. "As a new Scout, I remember asking, 'Prepared for what?' I will never forget my Scoutmaster's answer." The governor paused for a moment.

"He told me to be prepared for whatever comes along. I argued with him. 'How can you prepare yourself for everything?'

"He told me, 'Being prepared isn't limited to specific problems like packing a rain suit just in case you might need it. Being prepared encompasses a physical, mental, and moral readiness to deal with any old thing that comes along.'"

The governor lifted a glass and took a sip of water. "Today, we are here to honor Fortney Curtis, a Scout who was prepared." The governor recounted the events of the disastrous weekend and praised Fort's actions.

Fort's mouth felt dry, his nerves tingled, and his insides tightened. He hoped the governor didn't expect him to say anything.

The governor turned to Fort and asked him to stand next to the podium. "Fortney Curtis," he said, "at grave risk to yourself, you exhibited great initiative and courage to help the victims and to facilitate a rescue. On behalf of the Boy Scouts of America, I present to you the Boy Scout Honor Medal for your outstanding bravery and resourcefulness."

The governor pinned the award on Fort's uniform, shook his hand, and turned back to the microphone. "Fort," he said, "I understand you have joined the local rodeo team and are doing quite well. Which event do you like best?"

The governor's eyes twinkled as he stepped back from the microphone.

Fort looked at Tana Newton. The grin he saw on her face confirmed what he had already suspected—she had set him up.

He smiled as he leaned closer to the microphone. "My favorite rodeo event," he said to the hoots of laughter that had already started, "is bull riding."

About the Author

As Scoutmaster for his sons' Boy Scout troop for four years, Mike Klaassen enjoyed dozens of monthly campouts in Kansas. Weather conditions ranged from hundred-degree heat to ice storms. He also participated in four summer camps in Colorado and two ten-day treks through the Philmont Scout Ranch in New Mexico. In 1999, he received the Scoutmaster Award of Merit from the Boy Scouts of America and the National Eagle Scout Association.

After a frustrating trip to local bookstores to find novels that might interest his teenage sons, Mike decided to write stories himself. *The Brute* is Klaassen's first novel.

Mike grew up on a farm near Whitewater, Kansas. After earning a degree in accounting from the University of Kansas, he became a Certified Public Accountant and worked for six years in public accounting. An interest in investments led him to a career as a stockbroker and Certified Financial Planner. After thirteen years in investments, including five years as branch manager of the Wichita office of a major brokerage firm, he became Chairman of the Board of the local bank his father co-founded.

Bonus Features

It's not your favorite premium DVD. It's a Blue Works novel for young adults. We pack every Blue Works novel with "extras" because our books are created at premium quality — no wasteful mass-production, no newspaper print pages, no formula stories. With every purchase of a Blue Works novel you'll receive some or all of these incredible features:

Downloadable from our webcenter:

- A full-color poster.
- An extensive study guide written by the author.
- A "Making Of" interview with the author and others.
- Deleted or extra scenes not found in the novel.
- Fan-fiction links where readers take the story further.
- A limited edition, official trading card for the book.
- A full-color bookmark, door-hanger, club card and more.

By sending us your purchase receipt:

- An autographed Blue Card™. This archival-quality, deep blue, luminescent, mica-speckled card is hand-signed by the author.

www.windstormcreative.com/blueworks

Blue Works
Attn: Bonus Features
c/o Windstorm Creative
Post Office Box 28
Port Orchard WA 98366

For a partial listing of other great Blue Works novels, turn the page.